Bound

Dark Fae Prince

Amy Horikami

ISBN: 9798833363744

Imprint: Independently published

DEDICATION

To my girls: may you always stand up for what is right.

Chapter 1

DEVRON

As if I had anything better to do than spy on my cousin. He was, after all, supposed to get married today to some simple human girl. All part of the noble alliance they had with this pathetic town of Retna. I was here to see what unfortunate girl was getting trapped with the King of Llor, at least that is what I told myself.

Really, I was just avoiding my brother, Kadrell, the Dark Fae King of Bethrel. When he offered to have me spy on our light fae cousin, I accepted. Being second in line gave me more freedom to roam, at least when my brother was not trying to rally me into his dark undertakings.

Grateful he at least let me have my own stronghold on the border that connected to the ogre lands.

I stayed there most of the time with my men and ruled that lower part of the kingdom under his jurisdiction. My powers made me an ideal match for any invasion, along with my skilled men. While the throne belonged to my brother, my power all made up for it. I was stronger than any other fae, a weapon in and of itself, something my brother liked to use to his advantage. I hated it. It often reminded me of the past and the awful deeds I have done. I was tired of his games though, hence why I gladly accepted his offer to come and get away from his firm hand.

We have been here about a week and set up camp just outside of Retna, along with the other caravans. Our dark vardo was compensation from a side excursion with a sorcerer on our way here.

We aided him with a troubling set of bog pixies that were ruining his herbs for enchantments.

He was furious when we accidentally trampled his precious herbs while capturing the bog pixies and started to berate me and my men. My pride got the better of me. Once I found out he was heading here to Retna, I took his wagon. Deciding he could venture here on foot instead.

I reached up and rubbed my shoulder where one of those pesky verminous creatures bit me. Luckily, it was fully healed thanks to my fae magic, but those poisonous, sharp, little fangs sure left an impression.

I had my men keeping an eye out in case he decided to grace us with his dreadful presence. It has been over a week with no sign of the sorcerer, so he must have decided to stay put. Twenty miles was a bit far to walk, even for one who possessed magic.

"You okay, Your Highness?" my second in command, Nor, asked as he joined me by the fire next to the run-down wagon. I turned and looked at the older fae, who was taller and broader than most, with his head shaved bald, and muscles that would put most men to shame. Grateful he was not only my second in command but a friend. What I compared to in power, he matched in strength. He was the one who taught me to control my magic at a young age, along with the skill to fight. While my father's focus was on his heir, I was often overlooked as the second son. Grateful that Nor took me under his wing when a lost young prince needed an example on how to be a man. Sadly, I failed him more often than not and was grateful for his patience. I had too much of my father in me. The old King of Bethrel was a prideful man. Often bestowing cruel punishments to his subjects and found joy in tormenting others. My brother, now the king of our lands, followed in his stead. Our kingdom was suffering because of it and I could do nothing about it.

Grateful that when I started to turn to the ways of my father, Nor was there to set me straight. He was more of a father figure than a friend. He helped me grow into my role as prince of our kingdom, at least in the little area I had jurisdiction over.

Shaking my head, I said, "Just thinking about the journey here." He squatted down and sat on our makeshift chairs, which were wood stumps my men had cut from nearby trees. He turned to the wagon, then looked back at me, and grunted with eyebrows raised. I felt a lecture coming on. I stood since I was not in the mood for being lectured, knowing I should have just turned the other cheek and left when the sorcerer started yelling at me and my men. I could tell he was disappointed that I stole the wagon, and if I was honest, so was I. My pride prevented me from showing it though and I was grateful he didn't press the matter.

He often tried to teach me to serve those without expectation of anything in return, that is what a true monarch did. Like the light fae king that I was here to spy on, but I was no king and I definitely wasn't a light fae. Dark Fae blood ran deep through my veins, along with the tyrannical line of reigning royalty. I couldn't change who I was, but for some reason Nor believed I could, and guilt settled in my chest at the constant failure I was to him.

"I think I'll go into town and see what trinkets these humans have come up with to sell. Tell the men to keep their eyes open for my cousin, and report anything suspicious. They are not to mingle with the townsfolk, we are here to observe."

"Yes, Your Highness." He bowed, then walked away to communicate with my third in charge, Captain Brenon, about what the men were supposed to do. Brenon was the opposite of me; very calm and quick-minded, which is why I quickly promoted him to be in charge. Him and Nor were great assets to me and my men. I trusted them both with my life.

Wrapping my cloak around me and lowering my hood to keep my identity hidden, I headed out of the temporary camp and into the busy town.

People were bustling in and out of shops and homes getting ready for the festival. Banners were being hung from house to house. Baked goods being sold on every street corner. An older gentleman was playing the fiddle ahead of me in front of the fountain that made up the center of the town. His hat was placed on the ground in hopes to gain a few coins for his talent from those passing by. The song he was playing was jovial and children gathered around to dance to the merry tune, hooking arms, and spinning to their heart's content.

"Come on Helen!" came a voice to the right of the fountain. A young woman with auburn hair was pulling her friend, who must be Helen, into the area where the children were dancing. *Helen, it fit her perfectly.* The thought shocked me since I did not have time for such things. I quickly put such nonsense aside as another girl with dark brown hair came up beside them. She seemed lost, as if she couldn't decide to help her friend join the fun or to tell the other one to leave her be.

"I can't, Claira. It isn't proper," she playfully scolded me while rolling her eyes. Claira returned the gesture.

"Come on Lillian, let's show my cousin what fun we can have." She looked at the brown-haired girl, who still seemed lost at what to do.

"Fine! I will dance by myself." Then she skipped to the middle of the square and started twirling and moving among the children, but shortly after, she headed back and grabbed Helen's hand to pull her in. A smile so pure and bright came to the girl's face as they spun together and laughed. My heart stopped at the sound that escaped, the one named Helen's, lips. It was angelic and I was entranced. Who was this young woman and why was I so drawn to her?

My feet must have moved of their own accord since I found myself in the center of the square watching them. They spun closer and closer to me until the next thing I knew, I was stepping in between them. Her friend, Claira, let her go so she could spin away from her arms and when she spun back, it was in my arms that she landed. A gasp escaped her lips as she realized it was not her friend who held her now. I tightened my grip on her waist and spun her around the square, silently hoping the music would never end. We weaved through the children, as they still danced around us to the fiddler's music. Not even aware of what was happening.

Not knowing what overcame me since I never danced, not that I didn't know how, but when balls and banquets were held at the castle, I avoided it at all cost. Something about this girl drew me in and I've never been more eager to dance with someone before. As I looked into her wide blue eyes, twirling her around the fountain, I could not help the smile that formed on my mouth. Realizing I have not felt this kind of joy in a long time. It was so refreshing and new, I didn't want it to end. My current life was so full of darkness and regret. My smile brought a flush to her cheeks and something stirred within me.

After a few more minutes the music ended but my hold on her waist did not loosen. Maybe he would start another tune and I could continue to dance with this enchantress in my arms, for what other person could place this spell upon me.

Giggles came from the side and I looked up to see her friends staring at us. I released her immediately and gave her a quick nod, then turned and hastened down the path that led out of town, not knowing what overcame me in those few minutes. I was only a few steps in the direction of my destination, I could not help but turn to get one more glance at the girl. Trying to convince myself it was just to make sure her friends returned to her and not because I was drawn to her for some unknown reason. To my surprise she was still standing in the same spot I left her, staring after me. I could not help the small smile that graced my mouth. She returned the gesture, and my heart soared, knowing I put it there. Her friends suddenly swarmed her and started giggling and pulling her in the opposite direction of me. She followed but looked at me still as they dragged her to the sweet shop nearby. Once they came to the doors that led to their sweet indulgences, I turned and fled before my feet decided to follow them there too.

Chapter 2

DEVRON

As I walked through the encampment to our humble wagon thinking about the dance I just had with a dark-haired beauty, I heard a commotion coming from our site. A middle-aged woman with blonde hair tied up into a chignon was talking to my guards with one hand on her waist and the other pointing fingers at my second in command. I hurried forward to settle whatever was going on, grateful that even though Nor looked irritated, I knew he had the patience of a lamb.

"Don't tell me he's not here! I see his wagon plain as day, you big oaf!" Then she jabbed a finger into Nor's chest. Shocked that she had the nerve to touch him since he was three times her size.

"What's going on here?" I ask Nor, stepping up beside them. She turned to me immediately. A look of relief came over her

"There you are, Sorcerer! I need your help but this big imbecile keeps telling me you are not the one I'm looking for."

She was right. The man she was looking for was twenty miles west in a little cottage with a ruined patch of herbs. I couldn't tell her who I really was and ruin my cover so I decided I would try to redeem myself and help her as the sorcerer hopefully would. Without giving away my real identity of course.

"No need to fret, Madam…?" I paused, waiting for her to finish the sentence with her name.

"Taylor, Madam Taylor."

"Yes, Madam Taylor, how can I help you?"

She suddenly became hesitant as she looked at my men gathered around us.

"Could we…maybe…go inside? It is a delicate subject." She asked me, then looking at the rundown wagon, hinting at the place she wanted to have our private conversation.

"Sure, right this wa,." I told her, sweeping my hand out towards the wagon. Nor followed and right before she stepped up, she looked at him and then at me with raised brows. Quickly I pushed my annoyance down before I offered her a snide remark. As if she had authority about who could be alone with the dark fae Prince.

"No need to worry. Nor is my second in command and anything you say to me is safe with him." Raising my brows in return, daring her to retort.

Sticking up her nose she gave a loud "Hmph!" of disapproval.

Even if she did not like the situation, she would either accept it or go find the actual sorcerer who was still in his swamp. I had no problem dismissing this insolence, even if it blew our cover. I had more important things to do than entertain snotty old women.

"I didn't realize sorcerers kept guards around." her voice full of suspicion.

Since Fae couldn't lie and so far I got away with not telling her I wasn't the sorcerer she was looking for, so I scrambled for a true statement to tell her.

"I'm not sure what sorcerers keep, but for myself, I have a guard." Leaving it at that, I motioned her once again into the dark wagon trying to avoid any more interrogation. She nodded, accepting my statement, and proceeded up the steps to my relief.

She went directly to the small table in the corner and sat down. She was bold. If she knew who I really was, a royal prince, she would have waited until I told her to sit. Taking a deep breath, I let my pride go. This excursion to find out about my cousin's bride was turning into more of a burden than a relief. Making my way over I sat across from her on a small wooden stool. Nor stayed by the door, looking outside the window guarding the wagon, while making sure the rest of my men were doing their duties.

So, what can I help you with?" I asked her again hoping this was quick. I had a king to spy on, but all I could see was a blue-eyed beauty dancing in my arms. I shook those thoughts from my head. I could not get distracted.

"You see, I have…a problem."

She begins to tell me how five years ago I helped her brother-in-law with his orchards, well the sorcerer I was feigning to be, helped them, making them produce beautiful fruit every year. Not realizing how this was a problem I had to force my reaction to her statement down. Where I came from food was scarce as it is. She should feel blessed.

"They are prospering, and I am left with the tail end of it. I have a husband who is worthless, when I should have married his brother."

This was not really about the orchard at all then, and I was somewhat intrigued. She was here over a dalliance? Continuing her tale of how her best friend stole the love of her life and cheated her from living a life of luxury. I wanted to roll my eyes but prevented myself from following through with the action. She was just bitter that life did not turn out how she planned. I scoffed inside. She knew nothing about the hardship of life. I was getting bored quickly, not that I already wasn't, I decided to hurry this conversation along. Thinking I should just throw her out and have her deal with her own problems.

"I'm not sure how I can help you with this delicate situation. As you can see, I'm dreadfully busy and it seems like a family matter" trying to sound sympathetic, but my sarcasm accidentally slipped. Standing up to tell her the conversation is over, I motion her towards the door. Needing her out of this wagon because I had a king to find.

"I want them gone." She stated bluntly, realizing I was dismissing her. I was confused at first. Gone from town? Gone from...

She must have noticed my confusion since she repeated her statement. "I want them gone. They don't deserve the life that was supposed to be mine! Having to look at their child every day, and my own, who only looks like her wretched father! Give me a potion, poison, anything!"

Was this woman mad! I wasn't going to help her get rid of someone, let alone her own innocent family because life didn't turn out exactly as she hoped. Stealing a wagon was one thing, but killing innocent lives. I already had enough blood on my hands from my brother's manipulating ways.

"Well, can you help me?" she demanded and had the gall to tap her foot on the rotting wood below her feet. I had to push my power down as it rose in my body. It was demanding to release justice on this woman, her behavior towards me, and the harm she wanted to cause others who she *thought* betrayed her. I will admit I was prideful, arrogant, and even a trickster at times, but I was not my brother. I've come so far to squash the carnal tendencies that plagued my family. Nor had taught me from a young age that life was valuable, while my father showed no mercy to anyone who crossed him, my brother sadly following in his stead.

Taking a deep breath and turning to Nor for help. Only I could tell he was astonished at the current conversation by a slight raise in his eyebrows. After a few moments of hesitation, she spoke once again.

"You're not really the sorcerer, are you?" She asked, then fear entered her eyes realizing she told all her malicious plans to the wrong man. "You worthless piece of scum!! Preying on innocent women! I'll make sure everyone knows who you really are! How dare you!"

Light blue power was tingling at my fingers. She stepped back, now trembling with fear, realizing her mistake.

"How dare you! Do you know who *I* am!" I hissed at her, my body raking with power. No one talked to me that way, I was a prince, royal blood ran through my veins, I had enough of her. I wasn't the one who came strutting in and demanded I help her with her evil schemes.

"Your High…sorcerer" Nor addressed me. I turned to him quickly. He stepped forward and placed a hand on my shoulders. A look of reassurance shone in his eyes that helped calm me down. I was better than this. I took a deep breath and nodded towards my second in command.

He didn't take his hand off my shoulder as he turned towards Madam Taylor.

"We will help you." He told her. I could not believe my ears. The man who has taught me life was valuable, to be the opposite of everything I was forced to be, was now agreeing to help this madwoman. I started to protest but he turned to me and squeezed my shoulder gently in a reassuring gesture. I nodded, putting my trust in him. He never failed me before.

"Good." she expressed with her head held high, arrogance once again swarming around her. "I also trust that what is said between us will be kept confidential."

I didn't want to promise this woman anything. So, instead of saying 'yes,' I simply moved on to our deal.

" Now, if you will follow me, we'll get things taken care of." Nor motioned for the woman to exit the dark wagon and follow him.

I watched them exit, not believing what was happening. This couldn't be the man who practically raised me and was now helping this cynical woman with her plot for revenge. Once she was down the steps and waiting to the side, he came back through and approached me. He towered over me as he grabbed both my shoulders and sighed, then turned to look out the cracked window. Madam Taylor was impatiently tapping her fingers on her folded arms as she waited for Nor to return.

He turned back to me and leaned in whispering "We can't have her knowing who you are, I'll take care of everything."

I pinched my lips. I didn't want blood on his hands either.

He gave me an assuring smile. "Trust me, have I ever steered you wrong?"

He was right, we could not be discovered. If word got back to my brother, the king, who knows what cruel punishment he would deal out to me and my men. The scars on my back stung with a phantom pain just thinking about it. He was just like our father and desired perfect obedience. No room for error. While he never actually followed through with his threats of punishment, at least to me. The people I had jurisdiction over in Grauntrea and my men suffered at his hand. My father was a different story. He required ultimate submission and obedience no matter the relation. The jagged scars on my back proved that even his own son had no room for error. Too many times have I felt the whip from his own hands, and it was those times that Nor was the one who nursed me back to health.

Emotion swelled within me for this man who has always looked out for me when no one else did. I nodded to him, trusting he would do what was right.

"Get ready for tonight. We have a festival to attend and a report to bring back to our king."

He turned and left the wagon. I watched through the window as he guided the madwoman away from our camp. He was right, I had to stay focused. I headed out of the wagon to gather my men so we could plan our strategy for tonight. Maybe, If I was careful, I could slip away from my men during the dancing. Who knows, maybe a blue-eyed, black-haired lass would end up in my arms again. I secretly hoped she would.

Chapter 3

HELEN

"Are you going to the festival tonight?" Claira asked Lillian and me from a low branch that was above us. After we made our way through the shops in town and picked up sweets from the bakery, we headed to the orchard to relax. We finished the delicious morsels before we even reached the edge of the blossoming trees. Both our fathers, who were brothers, had shared ownership of the apple orchard and we spent many of our days here as friends. While Claira and I were cousins, Lillian made our trio of friendship a tight knit group.

"I'm not sure? It depends on my mother." I responded. I hoped she would. She has been moodier as of late and I've been tiptoeing around the house for fear of setting her off. Father stayed locked up in his study most days with work, which only left me to deal with her emotions.

"Hmmm," Claira mused. "I wonder what would persuade her? She has been so uptight lately."

Little did she know.

"I know, maybe my father can have a say in it. He does have some authority as the overseer, *and* since you are a young maiden, it *is* required to present all those in town who are eligible to be a bride."

She was right, every eligible maiden who was eighteen was required to attend the festival. I was only seventeen though. My birthday was next month and therefore, I was not required to attend. None of us were. We all had a few months until our birthdays. It is one thing that made us close. We were all seventeen and practically grew up together—birthdays within three months of each other.

"We aren't quite eighteen Claira," I lightheartedly chided her.

"Oh, what's a couple of months? Don't you wish to see the fae? I hear the men are so handsome and tall." She swooned from her branch, putting the back of her hand to her forehead for effect. We all chuckled.

My thoughts jumped to the mysterious man who danced with me earlier. They mentioned the incident that happened this morning when we entered the bakery by saying he was probably the fae who came to choose his bride and I would be chosen. I denied it, but my mind wondered if the man actually was. I never saw his face, so I wasn't sure if the mysterious man who swept me into his arms to dance was actually one. His hood was pulled down low the entire time, not giving a hint to the hidden beauty or pointed ears the fae usually had. I did at least know that he was tall and strong. I felt it when he twirled me around with grace and ease. I should have been terrified by this secretive stranger dancing with me, but I wasn't. In fact, I didn't want the dance to end. I felt drawn to him in a way that I did not understand. Maybe, I will meet him again tonight. I hoped I would.

"What about you, Lillian?" Claira asked, interrupting my thoughts about the mysterious male.

I turned to my genteel friend. She was petite with dark brown hair, and was the quieter one of our little group. She shrugged her shoulders and picked at the grass that was around the edge of the blanket we were sitting on together.

"Watch! She'll be the one chosen." Claira playfully teased her.

"I wish." Our friend quietly responded with lowered eyes, her shoulders drooping.

We all went quiet. It was common knowledge not only among us, but the town, that Lillian was mistreated often by her father. He was the town drunk and sometimes in a fit of rage he would physically hurt Lillian. We couldn't do much to help improve her situation, but sometimes we would sneak her into our rooms on nights when we knew her father had drunk too much. Then, the next morning, before anyone else rose with the sun, we would sneak her back out. Just recently she became an assistant to the seamstress, which not only improved her quality of life, but provided some protection from her father, at least during the day.

I leaned over and wrapped my arms around Lillian and pulled her into a hug. She titled into my embrace and squeezed my hand as a thank you.

"I'm sorry, Lillian," Claira spoke from up above us. "I didn't mean..."

"It's okay Claira, I'm just glad I have you ladies here. No fae could ever replace the friendship I have with you two."

Claira hopped down from the low branch and joined in the embrace. I hoped nothing would ever come between us.

Evening was approaching and Mother was still not home, which was unusual. I wonder what kept her out and if she was attending to some important business.

In a way, I felt relieved since Claira was coming to pick me up for the festival. We decided that even though we were not quiet eighteen we could go and enjoy the festivities with the rest of the town. Mother didn't really like Claira for some reason and every time she was here, she snubbed her. One time she warned me to be careful or I would end up like her, which I disregarded. I knew Claira was more carefree than most, but I loved that about her. She was not only my cousin, she was my best friend, along with Lillian.

After my handmaiden, Trinity, helped me wash, dress, and style my hair, I headed downstairs to my father's study. I knew I would find him working on ledgers for the estate, since that's where he spent most of his time. Along with partial ownership in the orchard, other estates, and land, we were well established and among the wealthier of this beautiful little town.

Maybe that is why Mother was so irritable recently? She has been pleading with Father to move and set up our estates in another part of the country or town. He refused saying that Retna was all we needed. I am glad he didn't bend to her whims. I loved it here and the life it provided.

Knocking on the heavy wooden door that connected to his study, I waited for his response to allow me in.

"Come in."

I pulled down the handle and pushed the door open to see my father at his desk, surrounded by candles, looking over his accounts. He was tall with a straight nose and hair, styled short, was as black as my own. Most of my features came from him. My mother was quite the opposite, with blonde hair and a sterner demeanor, but that did not deter from her natural beauty I wished I had possessed.

"Oh, darling, you look radiant. Are you headed to the festival?" I am glad he approved. The light purple gown I wore was my favorite and was made by Lillian, too. Now that she was an assistant to the seamstress, I had her primarily work on my gowns since she had a talent for intricate designs and such. It also allowed me to spend time with her during the day. Occasionally, I slipped her a coin or two as a thank you. Anything to help my friend in her predicament. She would refuse, but I always insisted. She helped me find the loveliest fabric and perfectly fitted it to my tall frame whenever I visited the seamstress shops. The one I was currently wearing had long sleeves that opened at the ends, giving a flowing look. The neckline was round and cinched at my waist.

"Yes, I am. Have you seen mother? I haven't seen her all evening, and I wanted to get approval from her as well."

"I have not. I've been working on these accounts all day, but she mentioned she had some business to attend to. Don't worry, darling; you go and have fun. I assume Claira is going with you?"

"Yes, I'll be meeting her at the festival. The three of us decided it would be best to meet each other there."

"Stay safe, and take Trinity with you." Ah, yes, my handmaiden. I forgot, but I would encourage her once I was with Claira and Lillian to enjoy the festival. I hated having a chaperone over my shoulder. I understood my father's worry about the event. There could be dangers for an unchaperoned lady with how many outsiders come for it; not only to sell, but in hopes that their daughter will be chosen as the next fae bride. I wasn't too worried though.

After bidding farewell to my father, I left with Trinity.

As we walked down the path together, the sun was setting and I could see the town lit up before me as night took over the sky. The banners hung up with glowing paper lanterns attached to rope, made the town feel magical. Freshly cut flowers wrapped around poles along with many different colored ribbons. Shops were still open, hoping the excitement of the event would make the crowd's purse strings looser.

This was my first time going to the festival since I was too young to attend five years previously.

Music was already playing and the dancing began. As we entered the town square Trinity was immediately asked by a young man to dance. She was pretty, so it did not come to a surprise. She looked hesitant though, but I encouraged her to enjoy herself and that I would not inform my parents of her supposed neglect. Secretly hoping this would happen so I could have some freedom tonight. She thanked me and was soon twirling with the other fair maidens in the town square.

I looked around for Claira and found her next to my aunt and uncle, standing on a podium overlooking the festival. He was the town overseer, so his duties to the event meant leading the special occasion and making sure it ran smoothly as the chosen fae chose his bride. I made my way up to them.

"Helen! You came!" My cousin jumped up and embraced me once she saw me on the stairs.

I returned her hug and she looked around. I knew she was looking for my parents.

"Trinity is with me." I answered her unasked question.

"Oh, good." She beamed at me. "The fae haven't arrived yet and father is worried they are wanting to break the alliance. You came just in time to save me from their never ending worry."

She turned to her parents and told them we would be observing the dancing from below and dragged my body down the stairs behind her.

"Where's Lillian?" I asked my eager cousin.

"I don't know, but I'm hoping she comes soon."

I realized she was dragging me towards the dancing, and I stopped, pulling her back to me.

"Claira, I can't."

"Why not!?" she exclaimed. It's not that we couldn't dance, I was just nervous. The dance earlier put me on edge, even though I was scanning the crowd for a hooded figure, hoping I might figure out who he was.

"May I have this dance?" A soft voice came right behind me, and my heart fluttered at his voice.

Chapter 4

DEVRON

She looked lovely in her purple gown. I was watching her from the side in the shadows as the town started the festival. I was surprised they started the event since the fae did not arrive yet, which in and of itself was worrisome.

They were supposed to be here by the afternoon. I received many reports that there still was no sign of them and I wondered what kept my cousin from fulfilling his alliance with this town. It was a strange day, first dancing with a dark beauty, a mad woman wanting to get rid of her own family, and now my cousin being late for the festival, if he even was coming at all.

I took a quick scan of those in attendance at the festival and made note of any changes. Nothing. My eyes then searched for her. She was by her friend from earlier, Claira, if I recalled correctly. Noticing her handmaiden was no longer by her side and I scanned the crowd and saw her dancing with a young man. It seemed like the perfect opportunity to ask the young woman to dance. I shook my thoughts; she was too distracting. I was not here to mingle and dance like some infatuated simpleton. Yet, that is what this girl reduced me to.

Just like this morning, my feet had other ideas and I found myself making my way through the crowd. Where was my second in command? I needed someone to shake me out of this nonsense. Actually, knowing him, he probably would encourage it if we weren't on an assignment.

Soon, I was behind her and my palms started to sweat, my heart pounding. I pushed all those emotions down. I was a prince and this mere human…no…she wasn't just anyone, was making me feel things I didn't know were possible.

I took a deep breath and put on a charming smile. After all; I was the Dark Fae Prince.

"May I have this dance?"

She spun around, and a smile immediately lit up her face as she recognized me. My stomach clenched with anticipation. While she looked lovely from far away, but she was breathtaking up close. Her long dark hair pulled into an intricate style that blended with the night sky.

Holding out a hand, I was grateful she took it as I led her to where the other couples were dancing. My heart was pounding in my chest as I looked at her. No one's ever made me feel this way before. It was new and exciting, but also unsettling since I knew nothing could ever happen between us. I was bound too tightly to my brother's rule. The somber thought had me take another quick glance around. I noticed some of my men in the shadows, watching the festival, and no doubt me. They were hard to spot if you did not know what to look for. To the untrained eye they were just shadows. It was because I knew they were there and what to look for, that allowed me to see them. They were probably wondering what I was doing, dancing with this girl. I would make up some excuse later that I needed to get closer for when my cousin showed up and this girl provided the opportunity. I felt bad using her as an excuse, but if it kept me close to her the rest of the night then I felt justified.

Satisfied with my reasoning I pulled her close and looked into her eyes that were searching my own. I stepped into the rhythm of the dance and twirled her around the town square just like earlier. It felt so right having her here in my arms. She fit perfectly, as if she were made just for me.

I gave her half a smile but she returned it with cinched brows.

"What's wrong my lady?"

She seemed hesitant as she looked around then her eyes came back and studied the hood that shadowed my face.

"Who are you? Are you from around here?"

I chuckled, and picked her up at her waist to spin her around. She gasped but could not hide the joy on her face. I brought her down and close to me again, not missing a step in the dance.

"That is only for me to know." I told her teasingly, but my heart sank. She could not know who I was, now or never. Why was I even indulging in this dance that would not lead to anything. I was just setting myself up for heartache. Even if I could, my father and brother would never approve. She was human after all. Protectiveness came over me for this girl that I did not understand. I would never allow them to know about her. Too many times in the past have they used anything that I loved or admired against me. I learned quickly to hide my emotions around them as a boy. Always showing indifference to anything I liked.

I heard shouting to the side and turned to see what was happening. I could see over the crowd due to my height and noticed her friend from earlier was being protected by a man from an older gentleman. Recognition hit me and I scanned the area for my cousin. No other fae was here, at least from what I could see, but I knew they were. The man protecting her friend was none other than the Captain of my cousin's royal guard, Ronin. He was threatening the gentleman which I assumed was her father. I noticed she had a black eye and was shaking behind the captain as he stood in front of her protectively, not allowing the drunk man to touch her.

"Is everything alright? You seem distracted and worried."

I looked down at my partner and gave her a soft smile. I had to leave but I did not want to.

Having had a duty to fulfill since the fae finally arrived, I stopped and led her to the edge into the shadows, grateful she followed.

She looked behind her towards the dancing crowd then back at me. Her eyes were wide and I could tell she was nervous. I probably scared her with my dark and mysterious appearance. Good, it would make it easier for me to leave if I knew she feared me. My gut clenched at the lie I told myself.

I looked down at our hands that were still clasped together, never wanting to let go.

"I must go, but it has been a pleasure." I hesitated, then lifted my hand to tuck a piece of hair behind her ear. It must have come loose from our dancing. My hands tingling from touching her, made me want to touch her again, especially since I could see the blush rising to her cheeks. A small chuckle left my chest at the endearing sight before me. I was glad to know I was not the only one affected. Then bringing her hand up to my lips, I pressed them to her soft fingers.

"It has been a pleasure, my lady." Then I turned and left, needing to get as far away from her as possible. Not even caring that my cousin never made an appearance at the festival.

Chapter 5

HELEN

I watched him disappear right before my eyes as if he was the shadows themselves. Who was this mysterious man? I looked at my hand and touched the spot he pressed his lips against, it was still burning from his kiss. My insides fluttered thinking about his touch as he tucked the strand of hair from my face. I was disappointed I did not get his name as he darted my question with skillful distraction.

I did notice he had a ring on his pointer finger when we danced and kissed my hand. My insides fluttered at the thought of his lips on my skin again. It looked like a house crest of some kind. It had a symbol of a snake wrapped around a sword with rubies on the side. He must come from wealth to own such jewels. Maybe he was a lord visiting for the festival?

I could hear a commotion and moved from the dark alleyway to see what was going on.

Claira was running towards me through the crowd.

"Helen! They took Lillian!" she shouted to me as she shoved her way through the panicked crowd. Who took Lillian? I thought back on the mysterious man I danced with, but somehow I knew he wasn't part of the uproar that was happening now.

I moved forward to meet my cousin.

"Who? Who took Lillian? Is she okay?" I grabbed my cousin's hands once I reached her and anxiously asked her, hoping our friend was all right.

"She was chosen as the next fae bride!"

"But that's not possible. She's only seventeen!" While we all turned eighteen in the next few months, brides were *never* picked until they were of age. It was part of the alliance.

"I know! He even refused to pay the ransom to her father, saying he did not deserve it or her. Then he disappeared with her without even saying their marital vows." Then taking a big breath she finished.

"Which is why the town is in an uproar, they worry the alliance will be broken since the terms have not been met. Father is so worried, Helen! They don't know what we are going to do if we don't have the protection of the light fae. Most importantly…" She sniffed, and I could see tears glistening in her eyes which triggered my own. "What are we going to do without Lillian?"

My heart clenched for our friend and I grabbed her and brought her to me in a fierce embrace, hugging each other as we both shed tears over our friend. We always knew there would be a chance one of us would be chosen, but not today.

We thought we had at least five more years to enjoy our close friendship since we were not quite eighteen yet. Even then we figured we would all be married before that time approached and would live the rest of our days raising our families together.

Claira was right though, what was the town going to do? It was common knowledge the only way Retna survived against the ogre raids and the mystical creatures that roamed the nearby forest was because of the alliance we had with the fae. We let them pick a bride every five years and in return they protected our little town. Everyone knew we were getting the better part of the deal since the bride's family, of the one chosen, received a bounty of wealth in return.

With our grief consuming us we did not realize the festival had died down, and since Claira's parents were talking to the town council about the current circumstance we ended back at my house. Neither of us wanted to be alone as we grieved our friend. We often stayed at each other's homes throughout the years so it was nothing new. We passed the night away telling stories about Lillian. We laughed and cried about the adventures we always had as a trio. While we knew she was still alive, we still had a hollow place in our hearts since we did not know if we would ever see her again.

"At least she's safe." Claira sniffed.

"You're right."

We knew the hardships our friend went through with her ruthless father. So many times throughout the years Lillian would stay at either one of our homes to escape his intoxicated beatings.

"You're right," I said again. With that comfort that our friend was at least safe from her father, we talked about how she was probably attending balls and wearing the finest gowns, living a life that she deserved. Talking well into the night our eyes finally shut when the sun started to rise.

Chapter 6

DEVRON

It has been three days since the festival and I was pacing the throne room as irritable as ever. I could not stop thinking about the girl and how my life was chained to my throne and the dictatorship of my brother.

"What is wrong, Your Highness?" I turned and noticed Nor watching me from the doorway, a sympathetic look aimed my way.

"Nothing of significance," I stated and continued to pace, extinguishing the thoughts of her out of my mind. Instead, I mulled over the information my men gathered. It seemed my cousin made a friendly wager with his captain of the guard in a sparring contest and won, which was surprising since I knew Ronin was an expert swordsman. The loser had to choose the next human bride to keep the terms of the alliance. I scoffed to myself. As if they could really keep the raids from happening.

We had sort of an agreement with the ogres to stop raiding the villages and instead focus on their training to help in the future takeover of the Kingdom of Llor. My brother's plan was to dethrone my cousin and rule both lands. That is where I came in. While my power was common knowledge, I had another advantage not many knew about. Only my brother and my closest men had that privilege. Not only could I use my magic for myself, but I could also give it to others to enhance their strength in battle. I was a weapon and I knew it. The downside was when I shared my abilities with others my lifeforce energy drained quickly and it took days to recover.

I looked at my hands and the power they held, thinking that they were more of a curse than a blessing at times. As I stared at them my thoughts drifted to the beautiful hands they held recently.

How I lifted the dark-haired beauty and the pure joy she expressed as I twirled her around that night of the festival, wanting to give that to her again. I clenched my fists and trudged over to my throne, throwing myself down with frustration.

"Is it the girl?" my mentor asked as he made his way towards me. I turned away from him, ignoring his question. Facing the wall and brushing my hand through my hair, pulling at the dark strands. When I left Helen in the dark alleyway three days ago, I realized Nor was at the end of it and watched the whole exchange that happened between us. He didn't press me for answers…until now. Since fae could not lie I dodged answering and asked him one in return.

"How did you deal with the madwoman that came to our encampment?"

He sighed, this large man, who practically raised me. Knowing I was being difficult, but I could not face what I was at the moment and how it kept me from actually living the life I wanted.

"Well, since I'm not fond of ending innocent lives." I grunted in agreement, still facing the wall. He was a man of honor, even if his persona said otherwise. "So, I did a transformation spell on a dying couple at the infirmary and switched them with the ones she intended to end the lives of."

I turned to him. "What about the couple? Where are they now? Wasn't there a daughter?"

"There was no daughter present. I think she may have added that extra detail in hopes to gain our services. I placed them in a new kingdom far away and erased their memory."

I grunted in approval. While I did not agree with the extra effort he took, I would have probably just erased the memory of the madwoman herself and be done with her.

There was silence for a few moments, then he came up to my throne and spoke softly.

"While I know you do not think you deserve a life full of happiness, I know you do. You are not your brother or your father. You are a great fae who can make changes, and I believe…"

"What? That I am not a pawn in my brother's game! That I have the freedom to do and marry who I wish!" I sighed, "I am no great man. You know what I have done. My past is proof of that." The image of a little girl came to my mind and I quickly shook it off as guilt settled in. The past haunted me so much these days as invisible chains reminded me who I was. I did not deserve her; not her smiles, her dances, nothing. Dragging my hand down my face in frustration, I brought it back up to massage my temples to help get rid of the headache that was forming. How could two dances change me so much, and why was I affected so much by this young woman? Humans were considered beneath us, at least to the dark fae. The light fae changed when my uncle, the former King of Llor, married a human girl. It was part of the reason my brother wanted to take over Llor, to restore the fae to their fullest degree and have no more "human filth" as he would say, tainting our lineage that my cousin allowed to blemish his. Another reason I could never bring her here. I sighed again. It was a hopeless dream.

He bent over and grabbed my shoulders, looking me in the eye like he used to do when I was younger and doubted myself in training.

"Of course you do! You are made for great things Prince Devron. I see you tearing up inside every time you follow through with these raids your brother orders. Maybe we can find out who the girl is and…"

I quickly stood up, making him release me and step back.

"No! Enough talk. I am finished with this conversation."

I pushed past him, his mouth forming into a straight line as he gave me a stiff bow. Knowing I was disrespecting the man who practically raised me, but I was a prince, I had duties and obligations to fulfill no matter how much I detested it. I could not dwell on things that would never happen. This girl was pure, innocent, and I had nothing good to offer her. I lived in the shadowlands, where its king raided and plundered, leaving its subjects in darkness with me as the executioner that made it that way. The scars on my back were a reminder of why I submitted and why I was his pawn.

I made it to the door and grabbed its edge, as I bent my head down in shame at my outburst. I turned and saw my commander watching me.

"Forgive me." I softly told the man who, for some inexorable reason, has never given up on me.

He nodded letting me know he heard and understood, compassion filling his eyes. Exiting the throne room I went straight to my quarters, wishing I could change my fate and that she would somehow be in it, but it was not meant to be. I was no savior; I was the dark prince.

Chapter 7

1 month later

HELEN

I could not believe they were gone. I was holding onto Claira as she sobbed into my arms, my own tears streaming down my cheeks as grief overcame our bodies. It was nothing compared to my cousin's, who just buried her parents this very morning. It seemed there were so many tears shed the last month as we held onto each other for comfort through all that has transpired. Why was life so cruel and unfair?

Looking at the freshly placed dirt on their coffins, only reminded us that they were not coming back. I rubbed my cousins back, giving her the only comfort I knew how. At a loss for words that would heal the deep break in her heart at losing two of the dearest people in her life.

"Oh, Helen, what am I to do now?" She lifted her head from my shoulder and looked at me with red cheeks and endless tears streaming down her face. I pulled her back in and hugged her fiercely.

"You'll live with me, you silly goose," I said trying to lighten the mood, but a sob caught in my throat. "I already talked with my father, and he said he was already planning on it."

"They were so young and healthy. I can't believe sickness took them away from us so soon. One day they were up and about, then next they could barely get out of bed."

I knew what she meant since I was the one who helped her this last month to take care of her parents. They were so weak and delusional. They barely recognized us and often asked our names. Claira's heart broke every time it happened.

"Do you think in the end they remembered who I was? That I was their daughter?"

“Yes, no one could ever forget you, Claira, especially the loving and caring daughter that you were.”

She nodded and wiped her tears from her eyes and turned to look at their graves. I grabbed her hand and squeezed it. I hoped it would be okay. It had to be.

Chapter 8

5 Years Later

DEVRON

"Well, that was a disaster." Nor said from beside me as we rode together back to the town I haven't seen in over five years. We were heading out with a few of our men to Retna. We had it on good authority that the king was choosing his bride this time. I wasn't going to waste a trip if he was going to pawn his responsibilities off on to one of his men again, but I secretly hoped a black-haired miss would be there. Even though five years had passed, she still plagued my thoughts, and I hoped I might get a glance at her.

"Yes." Responding to Nor's comment on our failed exercise with the ogres. For the last couple of months, my brother ordered me to work with their army for our upcoming overthrow of the Kingdom of Llor. One I was not looking forward to. The ogres were incompetent, and could not follow orders, accidentally setting fire to one of my cousin's fields as we were scouting the land. Not only did it bring unwanted attention from Leon's soldiers, but it started plans for a fortress and barrier to be built around their borders. Which will no doubt put a damper on my brother's plans for overtaking Llor.

I hoped to delay him from finding out about our little mishap as long as I could, vowing my men to silence. They were loyal, so I did not worry. He was becoming more like my father, cruel and vicious, with each little mistake I made in following his orders. Most of the time it was outside forces that could not be controlled, but the punishment still fell upon me and those in my jurisdiction. Whether it was withheld food or the whipping of me and my men.

"I'm hoping the ruined exercise will not get back to the king's ears and we can redeem our mishap with information from the festival" I said.

"We can only hope, but we are loyal to you, your highness, so any slip of the tongue will not be coming from your men."

Then a smirk formed on his lips and I drew my eyebrows up in question at his change of demeanor. "Maybe you'll find your own bride at the festival, eh?" he teased.

"Leave it be, Nor. No one wants a prince who is a pawn in someone else's game. I have nothing to offer them. If my brother succeeds this town will no longer be safe from any foul creature."

I thought of her, and if it came to that I would steal her away to my keep. Anything was better than living under the cruel reign of Kadrell, even if the life was one of secrecy. He would no doubt put the humans in servitude with the blood bond once this town was seized. The dark fae were notorious for doing that to humans. A cruel and eternal commitment between slave and master. I never did such a thing to those in my keep, much to my brother's dismay. Those who dwelled at Grauntrea were free, and their loyalty came from love, not fear. Something Nor helped me understand at an early age.

Secretly hoping my brother would fail, I would not dispose of my men to die for this unjust cause. For months I have wracked my brain to come up with a plan that could ruin his chances, but I always came up short. While me and my men were strong, well trained, and a force to be reckoned with, the Dark Fae King had the numbers that would outdo any rebellion I conjured.

As we trotted towards the town I had reports saying my cousin found his fated mate. His ken'ora. Why did he seem to get all the blessed luck? Not only was it rare, but it was such a soul deep connection that not even the bonding ritual among the fae could reach that depth.

"You doubt yourself so much, your highness. The day is still young. Who knows, fate could be on your side."

I scoffed. "Whoever is in charge of my fate, must have abandoned my cause long ago."

"The only one in charge of your fate is you, your highness."

I didn't respond because I knew it wasn't true. My whole life was ruled by those above me. Yet, Nor still believed in me, always telling me I could make my own destiny and change the fate of our kingdom. I wish it were true.

"Let's get this job done, and we'll see how well fate assists once we report back to the king."

"Whatever your fate is, Your Highness, you will always have my loyalty."

What he said was true. Not because fae couldn't lie, but because he proved it time and time again.

"Thank you Nor."

We made it to Retna and stopped near the area we camped five years ago. The vardo was still there and abandoned. Apparently, the sorcerer never came to claim his rotten wood on rickety wheels. I ordered my men to scout the area before we set up camp to see how many light fae guards were already here and if my cousin came to grace us with his presence this time. He had to; you could not deny the pull of your fated mate. I latched my horses to the wagon and scouted around, observing those who came from nearby towns for the festival. Envy at their freedom to come and go as they pleased.

"Your Highness, look." Nor came up beside me and nodded to a figure walking towards me in the distance. "It's that madwoman again." In the distance, I saw the tall woman making her way through the crowd, her head held high.

I turned to Nor and raised my eyebrows, "I would seem fate is *not* on my side today."

He looked at me and turned back to gaze at the woman, shock, and then a smile overcame his features. I turned to see what else he saw. Did she bring someone with her this time? Behind her trailed a tall, dark beauty with blue eyes. My heart pounded in my chest. It could not be, could it?

It was Helen.

She was beautiful. Five years only enhanced that beauty, and I could not take my eyes off her.

"It *would* seem fate has found you." Nor grinned at me with a twinkle in his eye.

Panicking, I rushed into the wagon, leaving my second in command to deal with the women. I heard him chuckle and I cursed the man for seeing right through me. I was a coward and I knew it. What was wrong with me? It's not like she would even remember me. I had my hood down the last time we met as the memories swarmed my mind. I fought demons for goodness sakes, yet I was acting like I met one, which made me think of the madwoman she was with. Was she in trouble? I immediately regretted hiding in the wagon and made my way to the door to help release her from the cruel woman's grasp.

There was a loud knock on the wagon door, and I froze. I stealthily looked out to see my commander had abandoned me to deal with these women by myself. Curse him.

I pulled down my hood and took a deep breath to calm my nerves. I would play the part, and none would be the wiser.

I opened the door to what was supposed to be fate.

Chapter 9

DEVRON

"Well, hello, Madam Taylor." I said in the slyest voice I could muster, hoping not to give away my nerves. A gasp came from behind her and it gave me an opportunity to look at her.

"Well, what have we here? A beauty to behold, I dare say?" She blushed at my compliment and I loved seeing the color rise to her cheeks. Maybe, I could play fate to my advantage. "Have you come to bargain with her?"

Fear overcame her, and I regretted what I said. I did not want her to be afraid of me. So, I changed the subject and asked the older woman if the situation she found herself in five years ago had changed to her liking. Little did she know that her relatives were still alive and well, in some foreign kingdom. I had to hold back a smirk at the secret I held.

"Quiet, You!" Madam Taylor snarled at me, and my power surged in my hands at her disrespect, but I kept my features calm. I had self-control, and I would not let his woman get the best of me.

"I did not, in fact, turn out like I hoped," she continued, "Which is why I am here, and not to sell my daughter to the likes of you."

I must have misheard. This beauty before me was this vile woman's daughter? Protectiveness bolted through me to take this girl away from this woman, but I could not give away my disguise. Instead, I offered them inside to see what they wanted. The girl hesitated, and I wanted her to desperately know she was safe, just as she was in my arms five years ago when we danced. Warmth filled my body at the memory.

As she finally made her way up the stairs and into the confined area. I placed my hand on the small of her back and whispered that she was safe with me, giving her a small smile. That did not seem to hush her fears as a shutter went through her.

I hated that I made her feel this way and immediately took my hand away from her. She moved to sit with her mother at a table on the far side of the wagon. Once I reached the table they were now sitting at, I decided to take off my hood. Not only did I want her to see me, but maybe it would calm her fears to see a face behind the cloth.

As I did, I kept my peripheral vision on her, not wanting her to catch me staring. To my delight she blushed as her eyes roamed over my features, no doubt realizing I was also a fae. I knew our beauty was beyond human and I could tell she was captivated by my appearance, which made me swell with pleasure that she found me desirable, even if it was superficial. I drummed my fingers as I half listened to what her mother was saying, but she my attention when she mentioned she wanted her daughter to be the one to marry the fae at the upcoming festival. I masked the fierce protectiveness that surged through me. My cousin would not come near this girl if I had any say in the matter.

Then, something caught my attention with her story. It was her niece who seemed to catch the attention of the fae. Fate sure does have a way of returning justice, since I knew if she ever found out it was me who had a hand in her aunt and uncle's disappearance, it would ruin any chance I had to make her mine.

Maybe fate was on my side though, because my cousin would never choose her due to the bond he held with her niece. That gave some relief to my heart as I explained to them that he already found his ken'ora, and what that means to the fae. Fury shone through her as she confessed the injustice of it. I watched her daughter's reaction, hoping she wasn't a part of this plan her mother had stirred up.

As much as I thought she was beautiful I could not marry someone who would agree to this madwoman's schemes.

Marry? Nor was getting to my head with all his fate talk from earlier and I shook the thought out of my mind.

"Mother! How could you! Killing them because of spiteful jealousy!"

My fears subsided as I watched the exchange. She did not know about her mother's schemes. A weight lifted from my chest. Not that I was able to judge, I have done many things in my past that haunt me still to this day.

Maybe, Nor was right. If I played this intriguing circumstance correctly, I could not only redeem myself from my brother's punishment, but save the girl from this woman. I smiled. Fate *was* on my side.

"So, you are saying there is no chance my daughter could marry this fae?" she asked.

I smirked, “I didn’t say that.”

Chapter 10

The Next Night

HELEN

I was terrified as I ran away from the fae now sparring in the center of town square. Glad the fae who bargained with my mother stopped the marriage before I said my vows to the King of Llor, and changed me back to looking like myself again. So many thoughts were rushing through my mind.

I still could not believe my mother was the one who killed my aunt and uncle out of spite, leaving Claira an orphan. Tears streamed down my face as guilt gushed through me on how I treated her over the years due to my mother's manipulating ways. We were so close until mother turned me on her. Then disguising me as my cousin to use me to get the dowry given to the family by the fae. It was too much to take in with so much deceit. I felt light headed, but I did not know where to go.

I couldn't go back home to my mother and her vile ways. Was father also in on this plan as well? *No.* Shaking my head at that thought. He was always close to my uncle and grieved for so long after they passed, but maybe that was a lie too. Anger surged through me along with determination. I needed to find Claira, I did not know what they did with her, but I needed to set things right. As I ran along the pathway to calm my nerves and figure out a plan, I heard a commotion in the woods ahead of me.

I slowed down and cautiously walked towards the voices, knowing it probably was not the best course of action since it was dark and I could not see what lay ahead of me. Thoughts that it might be where Claira was held hostage was the only thing that pushed me forward.

Delicately stepping on the forest floor as I made my way towards the voices. They got louder so I carefully went from tree to tree making sure I was still veiled by their branches, not wanting to get caught when I just escaped. I could see the meadow up ahead and realized it was the encampment my mother took me to previously to make a deal with the wicked fae. I hid just beyond the trees where I could see the exchange happening between the dark fae and the king, realizing they were talking about Claira.

"I'll trade her for her cousin."

I gasped. The dark fae was bargaining for me, why? What did he want with me? I put my hand over my mouth, realizing my outburst was a mistake as he slightly turned and looked towards the trees where I was hiding. I leaned closer into the dark shadows of the forest hoping and praying he did not see me. He turned back to the argument at hand, and I slowly moved farther away from the exchange happening between the two fae.

I could not be found out. After years of being manipulated by my mother, and now I was being used as a bargaining tool by those same people who were supposed to protect me, I had to hide at all cost. While I knew I was not guiltless for how I treated my cousin over the years, it did not stop the deep betrayal that sunk into my heart thinking about how my mother ruined so many lives. Forcing back the tears from my eyes, since I knew if I started now they would not stop and I could not be discovered. Deciding to stay hidden and out of sight for a while, hoping they would not come searching for me and just leave our little town.

As the time passed waiting for the fae to leave our town, I thought back on how I didn't see the signs of mother's manipulating ways and the indifference I treated my cousin with.

-Couple months after Claira's parent died-

Claira had been here only a few months and things were going smoothly. She still mourned her parents and I did all that I could to distract her. I heard a knock on the door and thought it was Claira coming to talk with me, like we did every night before going to bed. It helped her sleep better as we told stories about Lillian and her parents, trying to remember the good times. We also planned for our future and talked about the eligible men in the village, dreaming of future weddings and families.

I went to open the door and was surprised to see my mother.

"Hello Mother, is everything all right?"

"Yes, dear. I just have a few things to say to you." As she stepped into my room and closed the door behind her, I became worried since mother never came to visit me at night.

"Alright."

"As you know, your cousin has come to live with us due to unfortunate circumstances, but it has placed a burden upon us, that financially we cannot keep up with."

"Oh. Well, how can I help? I do not need any new dresses, or I can help more with chores if you need to let some of the servants go. I could get a job at the seamstress since Lillian is no longer working there." That thought brought a wave of grief at losing my friend just months prior since she used to work for our town's seamstress.

"No, that will not be necessary. It is your cousin who should work for it. We are, after all, taking care of her."

"But mother, she is still mourning her parents. Give her time. We will work something out. Are father's businesses not prospering?"

"Not like it should." Which I knew now was a lie, but my young heart at the time was naive enough to believe the falsehood, even though evidence said otherwise.

"Oh." I responded as worry overcame my young heart.

"I may ask her to do a few chores around the house, just to earn her keep."

"I can help her. We will do it together and…"

"No, I don't want you to help her," She snapped.

"Why not?" Wondering why she was so defensive of me helping my cousin. I knew she wasn't fond of Claira but that was no reason to burden her with extra chores when she was still grieving. We still had servants to help around the house.

"It's not your place." Then she patted my cheeks, but it felt insincere and her smile false. "She has to earn her way darling."

Thinking of that conversation, I should have known my mother was up to something. I should have defended Claira more and called my mother out on her prejudices towards my cousin. Instead, I just helped Claira with her chores when mother was not looking.

4 years ago

Mother was right, Claira was a burden. The whole household was just dismissed because of her. Mother said we couldn't afford the extra help anymore because we had to pay for the extra food, clothes and other necessities for my cousin. My clothes were getting ragged since mother refused to buy me new ones, saying we didn't have any extra coin for such frivolous things, and what I had would have to do. My handmaiden, Julie, who I have had since I was a little girl had to find work elsewhere because my mother could not pay her wages. Anger flared within me. It was all Claira's fault. Mother warned me for months this would happen, but I never believed her. Now I am tired. My fingernails were brittle and my once fine dresses were worn out and stained from the extra chores and loads of dishes I helped Claira scrub.

I knew I was not getting out of this situation anytime soon. My prospects for marriage were next to none. Every time we went into town to buy produce and meat from the local markets, they all gazed at my cousin as we walked by. I have had enough. I could not live like this anymore. Mother was right. It was all her fault.

3 years ago

"Helen, why are you treating me this way? We used to be so close. What have I done to you to earn this treatment? Is it your mother?

"How dare you talk about my mother! You know very well what you have done. It is because of you that we are scrapping by. Do not play me for the fool Claira."

Then I knocked over the bucket she was using to clean the floors and stomped to my bedroom. I felt a tinge of regret as I looked back and saw tears in her eyes, but I pressed it down. I had to.

A sob escaped my lips at the memories of how I treated Claira. I was so wrong, and now I couldn't make it up to her since she was leaving with the fae, and I was stuck in these wretched woods with nowhere to go. How she must have hated me throughout the years with the cruel treatment I gave her .

My gut twisted with guilt, and looking back I now realized my mother did everything to have me on her side and treat my cousin with disdain. Anger filled me that my father, who did nothing about it. Surely, he knew. He was in his study most days reviewing his ledgers. He knew our finances better than anyone. He had to know, unless my mother's threats and manipulating ways made him a victim as well. She could have lied to him about our expenditures, just as she had done to me. I felt lost and didn't know who I could trust. Was everything I used to believe a lie? Mother had no problems using me to get what she wanted. She agreed to binding my tongue and disguise me to look like my cousin to marry a fae, just to receive a dowry. I could not go home, who knows what else awaited me and how I would be used to gain whatever else she wanted. Then there was the dark fae who just asked to trade me for my cousin. Why, though? What use was I to him? Dark thoughts plagued my mind on tales of how the fae used to treat humans. Determination and rage filled me as I pressed my lips together, waiting for a chance to escape.

I heard a twig break and stiffened. My eyes frantically looked around, searching for anyone that might have seen me. My heart was beating out of my chest as I berated myself for not escaping while I had the chance. Then a sly voice behind me said, “Going somewhere?”

My breath escaped my body and my heart froze as I turned. I was too terrified to scream and call for help. As I looked at him it seemed my body was paralyzed, I couldn’t move. Did he put me under a spell?

“Who are you?” my voice barely audible as fear choked me. I had to know the man who helped my mother with her scheme. “Why are you doing this? I have nothing to give you.”

“I just saved your life.” His cold tone pierced through me, as if I was supposed to be grateful for what he did. That brought my blood to a boil and my frozen heart now beat with retribution.

"Saved! You ruined it! You killed my aunt and uncle and tore apart my family." Sobs finally broke free, spilling down my cheeks as my shoulders shook, "my friendship."

"Not from where I was standing. Your mother was a vile woman who was killing innocent people, and using you to get whatever means she wanted!" he threw back at me, and I could see power from the fight earlier building up and wisping around his fingers.

He was right, no matter how much I wanted to deny it, but he was not guiltless.

"You helped her, you wretched man! They were innocent lives you killed! You murderer!"

"You know nothing! I may be cruel, but I am no murderer." He spat as his hands flared with blue wisps.

I didn't believe him. I saw my aunt and uncle buried all those years ago. So, if it wasn't him? Then who was it?

Realizing I may have pushed him past his patience as he continued to glare at me. My eyes moved to his hands and watched his power flow around his fingers. He wouldn't hurt me as well, would he? Even though he claimed he was no murderer.

I noticed a ring on his pointer finger. The powerful blue wisps gave light to the symbols carved into the metal. The snake carved around a sword lined with rubies that was so unique, I've only seen it worn by one other person. This couldn't be him could it? It was so long ago, but my young heart remembered the dances with the mysterious man who charmed his way into my affections. My own fingers tingled as it remembered the kiss he gently placed on them.

My eyes drifted back to the cloaked figure before me. We studied each other, and his eyebrows pulled into a scowl. I shook my thoughts. This could not be the man from that night five years ago. He was too cruel and cold to be the one who warmed my heart that night.

After a few moments, he closed his eyes, and pinched his nose, breathing in deeply. The blue wisps slowly disappeared, for which I was eternally grateful.

Knowing I should not push my luck with his newly calm manner, but I had to know.

"What did you do with my mother, and what happened to my cousin?"

Dropping his hand from the bridge of his nose, he looked me straight in the eye.

"Your cousin is safe. She left with the king."

"Are you lying to me?"

"Fae cannot lie." He pointedly stated.

I thought for a moment, wondering if his words were true. I heard rumors about the fae and their inability to lie, but along with those tales were their uncanny ability to twist the truth. Thinking about what he said, it seemed that it was all straightforward, I decided to believe him, to my surprise. Realizing I was just desperate for truth and he provided it to some degree. With my recent awareness that my whole life was built upon deception, I needed some stability, even if it was from this man. At least my cousin was safe, and from seeing her a few days ago it seemed the king loved her and I knew she would be taken care of.

Relief went through me. I wish I was safe. Then it dawned on me that if what he said was true, him denying being a murderer was also true. I put that in the back of my mind to think on later since I still needed to know what happened to the woman who caused all this.

"And my mother?"

"She's where she is supposed to be?" he growled.

My thoughts ran wild. He wouldn't kill her, would he? That would make him no better than her.

"Is she still alive?"

"Yes."

It was the truth. I could feel it. I didn't press for more information about her. The real question I needed answered made my palms sweat. I looked down to gather my courage.

"What about me? What is going to happen to me?" my small voice shook with anxiety. "Why change me to look like my cousin only to stop the wedding?"

I could feel his breath on my face as he stepped closer and hooked a finger under my chin, gently lifting my head up to meet his gaze. His hood was off and the moon was shining down on us through the trees. Its beams surrounded him, shining on his dark wavy hair that curled around his pointed ears. My cheeks blazed and insides warmed from his touch. I didn't know why I was reacting to him this way. I should be running for my life from this man. Instead, his dark eyes pulled me in and I could not look away. One side of his mouth tilted up and suddenly I knew this was the same man from the festival, it had to be. I wanted to ask him, but I didn't want that night of pure bliss that was so long ago to be ruined by this nightmare.

He started to lean forward and my breath caught in my throat, at the abrupt change in our circumstance.

"It was the only way I could save you. I'm sorry." He pleaded softly, his eyes showing a vulnerability I did not think this man was capable of. "Hopefully, one day you'll forgive me."

My heart softened, but his answer confused me. Save me? What was he talking about? I didn't have time to contemplate as anxiety swept over me and I became light-headed. I felt like I was underwater, drowning without being able to reach the surface. Then suddenly …everything went black.

Chapter 11

DEVRON

My arms quickly reached out to grab her as her eyes rolled into the back of her head and started to fall forward. With quick maneuvering, I turned her and put one arm under her knees and one on her back, lifting her up to hold her against my chest. My heart was pounding at her nearness and my body flushed as I walked out of the woods to meet my men where I told them to wait for me. It's not exactly how I wanted our first meeting to go since that time five years ago.

I knew she was hidden in the trees when I was negotiating with my cousin, but I wanted to give her a chance to show herself, and when she did not, I decided to take matters into my own hands. She was bold and fuming with anger as she asked me about her mother and cousin. I could not blame her, but when she accused me of murder though, my pride got the better of me. Little did she know what my commander did to keep her uncle and aunt safe. I'm glad for the training Nor taught me to reign in my powers when my anger flared. It was not her fault she had a deranged mother.

A surge of protectiveness went through me for this girl in my arms as I thought of her mother. I would never let that foul woman near her again. I had my men take her to the constable with proof that told her of all her actions towards her relatives. She was put behind bars to my great relief. I did not want her in my castle, rotting in my dungeons, that was too close since I was planning on taking her daughter with me to protect her. I pulled her closer to my chest and looked down at her serene beauty, her dark hair falling over my arms as I held her. At least I was able to apologize before she fainted. I could tell she was hesitant to accept it. At least she did not outright deny me. Hope swept through me that maybe we had a chance. The moonbeams shined on her face, and all I could think about was how perfect she was; her beauty and her spirit. It took courage to face the fae. My heart swelled within me. I hesitated at first then softly pressed my lips to her forehead, breathing her in.

I knew she was not mine, and doubted she would ever be. My heart almost tore at that thought, and I almost stumbled with the grief that swept through me, already mourning what would never happen between us. The thought of not having this girl in my life awakened a realization that she already stolen my heart. I doubt I would ever get it back. I pressed my lips again to her forehead and tried not to feel my heart breaking inside of me. I also had a resolve that no matter what happened, I would keep her safe.

Nor and my men came rushing towards me as I stepped out of the forest tree and into the moonlit glade, no doubt due to the girl who was faint in my arms.

I quickly told them the situation and formed a plan. I would open a portal and take her to our healers, while they would ride back with haste to Grauntrea, the keep I had jurisdiction over in my brother's kingdom.

With that being said, I opened a portal and stepped through with the girl who held my heart in her hands. Hoping I wasn't making a mistake.

Chapter 12

HELEN

I woke up to a pulsing pain in my head and reached up to place a hand on my forehead, hoping to soothe it. I could tell it was morning since the back of my eyelids were orange with light. At least, I thought it was morning. I groaned and leaned deeper into the pillow I was currently sleeping on. My thoughts were fuzzy but I recalled I was not in a bed when I fainted, but in the forest of Retna. I became alert almost instantly and shot up to see where I was. The large room was not my own and panic sank in. I was sleeping in a dark mahogany four-poster bed, with designs of flowers and forestry scenes carved into the wood. The carpet was maroon and there was a small fire across from where I lay. My surroundings shone with wealth and prestige. *Where was I?* Not having time to think on the question since nausea instantly swept through my whole body and the room blurred. I laid back down and took a deep breath filling my lungs, hoping to calm my queasiness, regretting I ever moved.

"It's alright dear, you just rest. His highness has made sure you have the best care," Came a soft voice to my left.

I slightly turned my head, not remembering seeing anyone in the room, when I quickly looked around, and opened one eye to peek at the person speaking. She was short, full-bodied, and had a caring charm to her. She was wearing a simple gray gown with a white apron around her waist and a cap that covered her gray hair. I noticed her ears as she turned to place a white cloth in a wash bin next to the bed. She was a fae. I wondered how old she was since I knew fae lived a long time but I thought they only had youthful appearances. Not that I have seen much of their world, since recently. Which meant I knew nothing, really.

She said his highness was making sure I had care. The only royal fae I knew was the one who married my cousin. How could I have gotten here, did that cloaked fae from the woods bring me to the castle? They seemed like they knew each other since they were arguing. Maybe that is why he bargained for my life, to make sure I was safe. Maybe, I misjudged him. It wouldn't be the first time in the short span of the last couple of days that I have done so.

The woman came closer and put the wet cloth on my forehead. The cool cloth immediately felt good and helped settle my nerves and stomach.

"You're a pretty little thing, aren't you. His Majesty brought me up from our village to take care of you. Don't have much women folk around since his mother, the queen, passed away." Then placing her hand over her heart as deep sorrow overcame her. "Bless her soul. She was a pretty one and I loved caring for the wee ones when she was alive. Now all the prince does is mostly train with his men." She chatted on as she moved about the room. I just listened with my eyes closed, not minding her voice. It brought a comfort feeling in this unfamiliar place.

"Maybe things will change. After all, being the second son and all. He deserves happiness, but here I am chatting away."

Second son? I'm pretty sure my cousin married the king. Where was I?

"Excuse me? Are we not at the king's castle? Is my cousin not here."

"Oh, I hope not. The King is a cruel one, miss. Oh, but I should not say such things. Don't mind me and my mouth. It will surely get me in trouble one of these days." She continued bustling about the room.

The king was cruel? *Oh, no! What have I done*? My cousin went from one cruel life to the next. I let out a groan of frustration. I would get us both out of this mess if it was the last thing I did.

"Here deary, take this. It will help."

She came up to me with a cup that had steam coming off the top. I raised my eyebrows and leaned back into my pillow, not feeling up to drinking whatever concoction she had for me.

"Oh, don't be difficult. I don't want His Highness thinking I didn't take good care of you now." I slowly sat up, and took the cup from her hands and warily looked at its contents and sniffed its aroma. It smelled delicious. Giving her a glance, I decided that I trusted her enough to take a sip.

"That's a dear. Now, drink that up, and I'll get your gown out and ready for the day. Now mind you, we'll have to make some adjustments since you are not as tall as most fae folk, not that I'm one to speak, but I'm quick with a needle, so no worries there."

"Excuse me," I asked before she went on to tell me more. Not that I minded her talking. In fact, it gave me a sense of ease in this foreign place with her friendly demeanor. "Where am I exactly, and…"

"Oh, forgive my manners, dear. I'm Mrs. Lynn. I'll be your handmaiden while you are here."

"Where is here, again?" I asked again.

"Why Prince Devron's Castle in Grauntrea. Don't you know? He owns this keep on the far side of the border, under the jurisdiction of the King, of course."

I did not know. I have never heard of Prince Devron. Did the light fae king have a brother?

"Is that the light fae king's brother?"

"Oh, no, miss. You are in the dark fae lands. Where King Kadrell, of the Kingdom of Bethrel rules and reigns. With a hard hand, I tell you too, but I'm not one to complain. No, miss, not me. I'm just grateful to be of assistance, here and all with you. Especially when his highness needed my help. Such a good boy he was, that prince."

The dark fae lands! They exist? Tales from my childhood when parents told their children about the dark fae who came and stole children to eat for their supper if they did not obey their parents. While it kept children in line, I did not think they actually existed. While we knew the light fae existed since we had an alliance with them, we thought they were the only ones. I swallowed the large lump in my throat. Fate was not on my side, it would seem.

"The dark fae lands?" I barely got out.

"Yes, dear. Oh, don't be fretting. I can see you have gone white as a ghost, but Mrs. Lynn will take good care of you. I, myself, took care of the young princes when they were just wee little things. Then they all went and grew up. Now, mind you, it wasn't my doing the king went cruel and all. Took after his father, but Prince Devron has the gentle hand of his mother. Runs this place with a fair hand, I tell you. Never wanting for nothing. Well, as much as he can provide of course. He still must answer to our king.

She shook her head, tsking. As she grabbed the cloth off my head and put a fresh cool one on.

“But you're safe here. Prince Devron is a good boy, I can see he be trying and all, especially with our keep and all who live in Grauntrea. While we may not have much, he does try.”

While she reminisced about raising the princes. I thought about what she said. I was in the dark fae lands, in a prince’s castle, and not with my cousin. She said she was my handmaiden. Was the man who brought me here some high Lord? Surely, he could not be the prince, not with the way Mrs. Lynn was going on about what a good boy he was. The man I knew killed my aunt and uncle and traded me for my cousin. I recalled when I accused him of murdering them, he became defensive and said I didn’t know what I was talking about, denying my accusation. Maybe, there was more to the story then I knew and I would just have to ask the man myself. Then there was my mother. My chest filled with grief at the actions she caused and I still didn't know where she was. All of these things needed answering. My head was pounding so much that I put those thoughts away so I could focus on Mrs. Lynn and her wealth of information.

"Now, I'll be leaving but coming back soon with some dinner for you. You just rest your pretty little head and know it's going to be alright." Mrs. Lynn interrupted my somber thoughts.

Would it be all right? I would think on it more later. Maybe this prince could help me reach my cousin so that I could apologize and find a way to make up for my actions towards her. I didn't know how I would do it, but I would try.

As I laid back down in the comfortable bed, my eyes instantly shutting as exhaustion took over and my body. I was more tired than I thought. At least I was safe. For now.

"Come back!" I yelled to a man in the distance. I started running through the forest to catch up to him, the fog so dense that I could barely see through it. It was cold, and I was shivering since I only wore a thin dress. I felt exhausted as I pushed aside the shrubbery and ran through the thick trees. I tripped and fell on the cold ground, my determination giving me strength to push up and keep running after him. A desperate feeling that I had to reach him before something horrible happened, that he needed me, and to my surprise; I needed him. This urgent feeling, sinking deep in my chest. I slowed down as I saw a large figure of a man laying on the ground about ten feet in front of me. I knelt down in front of him as tears streamed down my cheeks. I lost him, the man I loved. Sobs shook my shoulders as I turned him over. It was him! The fae who found me in the woods, but instead of fear I felt a deep longing for this man. I was surprised, yet, I wasn't. I reached down, and wrapped my arms around him and cried. I was too late.

Chapter 13

DEVRON

It's been two days since I brought her back to my castle. Right after I arrived, I sent one of my men to the village to find my old nurse who raised me as a young fae. I was grateful she was more than willing to assist me and be a handmaiden for the young woman now asleep in the guest chambers at my keep.

Which was where I was headed now. I wanted to see how she was fairing and if Mrs. Lynn needed anything else. I would give her all I could to make Helen comfortable. I reached her chambers just as Mrs. Lynn was walking down the hall, no doubt from just assisting her charge.

"How is she?" I asked the older fae

"What a dear she is your highness, young and pretty just like you said."

I didn't actually say that, but I didn't correct her as the truth of her words settled on my heart, warming my chest.

"She's sleeping now, the poor thing. Must have been through something awful, white as a ghost and trembling all over. Don't you worry Your Highness, I brewed her some of my healing tea and she should be sleeping now and soon be right as rain, I tell you, right as rain." She happily nodded her head.

"Thank you, Mrs. Lynn. I am sure she is very well taken care of under your supervision. May I see her?"

As we headed towards the guest chamber door, I started to think about how things used to be as a young boy before my brother started his royal duties with our father. Not even my mother could keep the cruel man from us any longer. When she passed away from an illness that was beyond our healer's skill, everything changed. Some say the Queen died of a broken heart, and I believed it. Father treated her just as he did everyone else in his kingdom. While she loved deeply and cared for her sons and all her subjects, my father was cruel and ruthless. Another reason I hated him. He took her away from me like he did with everything in my life. It made me grow up angry and bitter on revenge. Until Nor showed up.

It was the day of the accident that changed me forever. I was out in the practice yard by myself, with a sword I stole from the armory, my grief drowning me at what I just did. Hitting the hay-filled target with as much force and magic I could muster. I warped the sword and burnt the target. I continued throwing balls of pent-up magic at it, hoping it would make me feel better, but instead, it fueled my guilt, and fury ran through my veins at the monster I was. It started to rain, but I didn't care, I recently lost so many people I loved.

First my mother… then her. Rage surged through me as did my power. I remember being exhausted and my knees hitting the muddy ground in the practice yard. I heard someone come up to me and turned, seeing a tall burly fae reaching his hand out to me, giving me a soft smile. It was there that Nor started my training. He taught me to focus and control my powers, especially as it grew. To look for the good in the world and give more than you take. While my brother was being forged into the next dark fae king, I was being trained in the opposite. Even though for years I tried to be a better man, my faults surmounted any good I have done, which made me unworthy of this girl now recovering in my keep.

Mrs. Lynn softly opened the door up for me.

"She may be asleep, your highness, so keep it down and quiet ya here. I will not have the young miss jostled from her recovering." She reprimanded, then softly smiled at me like she used to when I was a young fae. "But I know you won't. You were always such a good boy and now a good man"

I didn't feel worthy of her praise, but I gave the old woman a small smile, knowing I could not change her mind. It was as if I was the young boy making messes in the nursery again and not the prince who ruled over her. She was always faithful to me and my upbringing as a child, no matter what I did. Nor and her were closer to me and taught me more than my own parents. I cared for them deeply, even though I felt I did not deserve their devotion and love.

Then I nodded to her, signifying I understood, before making my way to the girl's bed. She was asleep with her hair sprawled on the pillow; a white linen cloth placed on her forehead. Deep worry sank into my chest. *Was she also ill with fever?*

I lightly put a hand on her forehead, over the cloth. It felt hot, so I checked her cheeks with the back of my hand to make sure. She was burning with heat. I turned to Mrs. Lynn.

"She's running a temperature, what can be done?"

Mrs. Lynn hustled over to my side and placed her small hand on the girl's forehead.

"Oh, deary, her fever has worsened. I'll go get a tonic and be right back in a jiffy. Don't you worry, Your Highness, Mrs. Lynn will have the girl feeling better. Don't you worry, don't you worry." She kept repeating as she gathered her things and placed them in the basket. Then she left the room, leaving the door slightly ajar.

Realizing I was here alone with her now, and wanting to keep propriety, I turned to leave, only to be stopped by a sad moan as she tossed and turned in her sleep. My feet went back to her side on their own accord. Kneeling down beside her, I looked around seeing what I could do to help her. I felt lost at first, then I saw a wash bin next to the bed. I carefully took off the warm cloth from her forehead and dunked it in the cool water. Wringing it out I placed the cool cloth back on her forehead glancing over her features. She was beautiful. Her dark long eyelashes spread over her cheeks as she lay asleep. I looked around and pulled a chair up to her bed and sat watching her, convincing myself it was just to make sure she was okay.

I shouldn't be here. It's not proper. I reprimanded myself again, but I couldn't get up. I had to make sure she was comfortable, and I was just watching over her until Mrs. Lynn came back, it was my duty as prince over those in my keep, I rationalized.

Reaching out I gently took a straggling hair on her forehead, and tucked it behind her ear, then cupped her cheek in my hand.

"Ahem. Your Highness."

I quickly dropped my hand and turned to see Nor with a smile on his face in the doorway of the room.

I stood up as he entered the room. His smile only grew. He turned to the girl, and his smile immediately dropped, and worry overcame his features.

“How is she?”

“She’s burning with fever, but Mrs. Lynn just left to grab a tonic, so I decided to watch over her until she came back.”

“Hmmmm, I see, and you?”

“I’m fine.” I huffed out. I really wasn’t, not if she was sick.

“So it would seem.”

Needing to change the subject, I asked him why he was here. He handed me a letter with the seal of our kingdom in dark red wax. My brother.

"This just came in."

I grabbed the letter from his hands and broke open the seal with my finger, seeing what the King of Bethrel wanted.

I scanned over its contents, and I let out a frustrated sigh. I closed the letter and turned to Helen, still asleep in her bed, not wanting to leave her but pressing matters needed attention.

I turned back to my second in command, the smile back on his face, eyebrows lifted as he noticed my concern over the girl. I forced myself to not roll my eyes as I moved past him.

"Come, it would seem we will be having a visit from my brother soon and must pay for our slipup in training with our inept allies."

"Wait, Your Highness." Nor rushed out as he caught up with me. He stopped in front of me and placed one hand on my arm as he turned and looked at Helen.

"He must not know about the girl. He could use her against you."

"Against me? But she's nothing…" I couldn't finish the lie as I coughed and choked on my own bluff. I looked at her again. "She'll be gone before he gets here…hopefully." I redirected my statement, but I secretly hoped she wouldn't. I wanted her to stay. I felt a fierce protection over her unlike anything I have felt before. I sighed and turned back to Nor.

He raised his eyebrows and gave me a stern look. "Even if she was nothing to you, which I doubt."

I did not reject his statement, what good would come of it when he could already see right through me.

"She is still human."

I understood his concern completely.

"You are right. I will tell my men and the castle to be scarce when my brother comes. I'll make sure to keep Mrs. Lynn busy, and Helen stays hidden in her room."

I could not take any chances, not with my brother accidentally finding out about her. He detested humans and who knows what he would do if he found out I was taking care of this girl instead of forcing her into servitude for my keep.

"I know what she means to you, your highness. I may be old but I am not blind. Who knows, maybe fate will heal the both of you and together you will do great things for this kingdom."

"You think too highly of me old man, maybe your eyesight is not as good as you think it is," I smirked, trying to make light of the situation for my sake. "Who says she will even want me? My brother rules these lands. I have no say." I looked back at her again, a longing entering my chest. She was perfect and I was a prisoner to my own kingdom. It would never work, and no amount of jesting would take that away. I could not deny this feeling in my heart.

"Come, let us prepare for the king."

Chapter 14

DEVRON

Three days later, as I was pacing my throne room, waiting for my brother to make his entrance. Nor waited in a corner as a silent support, for which I was grateful for. I sent my men out to scout the town with my captain, Brenon, and Mrs. Lynn was still busy taking care of Helen, whose fever was finally going down to my great relief. I tried to visit her at least once a day, but she was always asleep. I never stayed since I was still afraid to face her wrath if she woke up, so I asked about her progress and went about my duties. Not visiting with her was for the best, I already felt guilty for bringing her here and then the whole ordeal with her family.

My thoughts were interrupted when suddenly the large doors to the throne room were thrown open, and an entourage of large fae in full dark armor came marching in. They were in two orderly lines, and when they stopped in front of me they shouted together a warriors cry. Then turning in perfect unison to face one another with legs spread apart and hands behind their backs in a warrior's stance. These were my brother's top ranked soldiers, and they had unyielding loyalty to him. They were a force not to be reckoned with, which is why he brought them when he visited. I could not outdo these fae with my magic when they were combined against me. I at least got the satisfaction that my brother knew what I was.

"Ah, my dear brother." A sleek voice came from a man with long black hair and broad shoulders. His black armor shined as he entered the throne room. Walking down the center of his men towards me in his grand arrival. Half of his hair pulled back and tied with a leather chord. An onyx crown with sharp pointed spikes placed on top. Looking every part of the fearsome ruler he was.

"It's been too long, Your Majesty." I bowed and did not lift my head until his feet were in my vision.

"Yes, it seems though it is not long enough." As he looks around my keep with disgust. "You know you could be wealthy and fix this hovel, *if* you followed orders."

I looked up to give him a reply only to be struck down with the back of his hand.

Pain pulsed through my cheek and my power surged around me as I lay on the floor. I quickly scrambled to my feet and touched my cheek, looking at my fingers now glistening with blood. I pushed some of my healing power towards the cut to stop the blood flow. His men now surrounded me with swords out and ready to defend their king. If it was just us, he would not dare lay a finger on me. His little posse made him bold. I brought my power close to my body, not letting my defenses down. I was tired of his games.

He stepped through his men, sword drawn as he pointed it at my throat.

"Your little mishap with the ogres. Don't. Let. It. Happen. Again." He told me through clenched teeth as he pressed his sword to my neck, causing a piercing pain. I could not pull back though, my pride wouldn't allow it and it may even incite more punishment from me.

He gave me a wicked grin and lowered his sword.

"All this power, wasted on the second son. You are weak and pathetic! Worthless just like father said!" he finished with a snarl.

"Aaarrgh!" I leaped at him, my blood boiling with rage and wondering why I was letting his words affect me now after so many years of harassment. His men grabbed me and held me back before I could even get close to my brother. Then using their combined powers, they sent a shock through me that dropped me to my knees, my back arching as it pulsed through my body in piercing pain.

"Liar!" I yelled at him as I pushed through their torment. I was not going to give up that easily as I tried to fight back, pushing my own powers out of me, trying to put up a shield. I made enough headway to loosen their grip on me and fling them off of my body where they crumbled before me.

My blue force whipped around me in rage, ready to strike. Ready to kill.

This. Ended. Now.

"Devron." I looked to the right and saw Nor with a pleading look in his eyes. "You're better than this."

I looked back at my brother and could see fear in his eyes. I could do it. I could end him. All this pain, all this torture would be gone. I would finally be free.

"Please, Devron." Nor begged. "This isn't who you are."

Then who was I? This power was the only thing I had? For too long it has been used against me and not *for* me. This magic should have been helping me break free, not putting me in my own prison. Why was the man who helped me heal through every cruel punishment my brother has ever bestowed upon me, now telling me not to end him. Why?

Then, the memory of beautiful blue eyes looking at me made me pause. I squeezed my eyes shut. No, I was not worthy of her, but I wanted to be.

I took several deep breaths, reigning in my power, and glared at my brother. His fear was replaced with a triumphant sneer.

"This is not over, little brother. Our agreement is still on. We wouldn't want anyone to get hurt, now would we?" He threatened, looking at

Nor. I had to push my power down even more. I was still on edge. Shaking my head slightly in response to his threat, I felt like a child being scolded.

He only let me have jurisdiction over this keep if I agreed to aid him when he seized my cousin's lands. I thought I could get away with years of preparation, hoping his dream would slip away as he realized it was impossible to take over their lands. The light fae outnumbered us one to ten, but sadly, his greed for power only grew to an unyielding ambition.

I really did not care about taking over my cousin's kingdom. In fact, I just wanted to heal our own. While I knew I treated my cousin with indifference and thrived on pushing his nerves past breaking point, as I did at the festival. He treated his kingdom in a way that made him and his subjects prosperous. I know, because of the years of spying on the King of Llor and his lands. People were happier, and the lands were fruitful. I tried to do the same with my keep over the years, and I could tell a tremendous difference in the lives of my subjects than those in the capital where my brother ruled, which is why I yielded when he threw threats at me. I cared deeply about my people and wanted them to thrive, not live in fear.

"Good." He spat. "I'll let this little incident slide this time, but you better be careful, little brother, you'll not always have your friends to watch out for you." Then he turned on his heel, opened a portal, and disappeared with his men in tow.

I sank to my knees, my head falling to my chest as despair took over. How could this tiny bit of prosperity last while my brother ruled?

Hands were on my shoulders, and I looked up to see Nor kneeling in front of me.

"You did the right thing." He squeezed my shoulders and brought me up to stand before him. "There will come a time when opportunity will present itself and all your restraint will bring peace to this kingdom. Not by force, but because it was the right thing to do. Any other way will only be seen as a pursuit for power."

I didn't understand. How could I bring peace to this kingdom without actually killing the King? His hold was too strong and his men were too loyal. Even I, the most powerful fae, had no control over him. Which brought me to make my decision that Helen could not stay here no matter how much I desired her to. It was too dangerous for her. If my brother ever found out about her, he would take her away from me just like Nor told me earlier. I could never let that happen and I felt my power building up again at the thought of her in his clutches. I had to make it right before I sent her away though. I could not have her thinking of me as the monster I knew she already was.

Looking to Nor, I gave him an order that would hopefully have Helen looking at me in a brighter light. "I need you to find her aunt and uncle. I know it was five years ago, but I need to set things right with her. Take Brenon with you and all the supplies you need. You were right, the longer she stays here the more danger she is in, but I don't want her to leave thinking ill of me, no matter how vain or selfish it sounds."

"Are you sure, your highness? I don't know if I can find them right away since it was so long ago. It may take weeks and I know you want her safe."

"She'll be safe for now. I'll take extra precautions and tell my men to stay quiet about the situation."

"I'll leave right away then, your highness. I will ride since horses hate being taken through the portal, but I will go in haste."

"Do what you must, and may the roads be in your favor."

He grabbed my shoulders again and brought me close in an embrace. "I hope one day you can see the man I see in you, Prince Devron. I am loyal to you." Then he placed a fisted hand over his heart and bowed, then headed out to accomplish the task I assigned him.

How could he say that! I was not a good man, I had so many faults, and one good act was not enough to redeem me for all the dreadful things I've done, but hopefully, it will redeem me in the eyes of Helen. If she didn't see me as the monster I knew I was, that was all that mattered. Then maybe I could plead with the King of Llor to keep her in his kingdom. At least she would be safe there. I hated to lose her though, not that she was even mine, but the thought of her leaving even if it was what was best, left a hole in my heart.

Needing to burn off the pent-up energy from my brother's intrusion and distract my sullen thoughts, I headed towards the training grounds. My men should be back soon, and some sparring would do me good.

Chapter 15

HELEN

My eyelashes fluttered open. My memory recalled that the last few days I was fighting a fever. Touching my hair and nightgown, they both felt clammy and damp with sweat. Realizing my fever must have finally broken since it also felt cool. Slowly sitting up, I saw Mrs. Lynn on the far side of the room. She turned around with a tray, and a smile appeared on her face as she hurried to my side.

"Oh, thank goodness you are feeling better. You gave us all quite a scare. Well, except me of course, I wouldn't let nothing happen to you, Miss, mark my words. I would brew a dozen more tonics to get you feeling better."

She set the tray down on my lap and I saw porridge, toast, and sliced up apples were spread across the wooden tray. I grabbed the spoon and scooped up some porridge right as my stomach growled loudly. I flushed with embarrassment since I didn't realize how hungry I was.

"That is a dear. You just eat and get your strength up. I brought a simple meal since you have not really eaten the last five days or so. The prince even came and checked on you. What a dear he is, always fussing about his subjects."

I've been sick for five days? The prince even checked on me? I hardly remembered anything that happened.

"Thank you, Mrs. Lynn for taking care of me. I didn't mean to be a burden to you. I know you probably had other things to take care of."

"Not at all. Not at all." She assured me. "I was more than happy to see to your every need. Now, no more talking. Eat up girl! Eat up! His

Highness will have my hide if you are not fit as a fiddle."

While I was sure the same man who caught me in the woods was the prince, I decided to ask Mrs. Lynn just in case he was a royal subject or Lord. Questions that burned in my mind needed to be answered and resolved. He was the only one who could do that for me.

"What does the prince look like?" I asked nonchalantly.

She stopped what she was doing and gave me a soft smile. "Oh, he is a dear. He grew up just like his brother, tall and every bit as handsome as the fae come. Kinder though. Yes, much more caring. His dark hair is shorter since he was always fussing about it when he was younger. Constantly begging me to cut it for him."

Then she gave a chuckle. "One time, I caught him trying to cut it himself when I told him no, gave me such a fright when he did. Decided to use garden shears since I hid my sewing scissors." She shook her head and tsked, then looked at me pointedly. "He is the one who brought you back, you know. Says he found you in the woods, faint and all. You poor thing, all alone and cold in that dreadful forest, but you are safe now and finally recovering."

It was him. I knew it! Safe though? I wasn't so sure. I still had too many unanswered questions. Why did he bargain for me? Did he need a wife? I could never rule these dark lands. I had to find a way to escape if there was one, but I didn't know the location of the dark fae lands or how I would even get home. While he denied he was involved with my aunt and uncle's deaths, I was still unsure. My heart knew it was true, but my mind could not fathom how.

I looked up and saw Mrs. Lynn bustling about my room. She was so kind to me, so different from what I expected from the dark fae kingdom. Looking around and noticing again the immaculate designs on the four-poster bed, the wall hangings and even the twirls in the bedcover. Everything was dark and mysterious, yet beautiful. It was fitting for the land I was currently in.

Mrs. Lynn poked her head out the bedroom door and called to someone in the hall. Six tall men wearing the same dark outfits carried large buckets of steaming water. Then five more followed, carrying a large tub. Placing it down by the hearth, they started to fill it up with hot water. When it almost reached the top, they stopped pouring and turned to leave. Mrs. Lynn followed them to the door thanking them for their services. She shut the door and locked it in place once all of them were gone.

"Now, let us get you all cleaned up. Maybe take a walk around the gardens? Fresh air always does one good after sitting in bed for a while. Don't you think?"

I nodded, slipped out of bed, and walked over to where she was. She was right, a bath would do me good. For the next hour she helped me get ready. I could feel my strength returning and was grateful I was finally feeling better. Soon, I was wearing a dark red gown of velvet and came down in an a-line shape. Its square neck and open sleeves were a style I was not familiar with but was beginning to love. She finished by pulling my hair up in a simple style so it was off my shoulders and out of my face.

"Now, don't you just look beautiful. I knew that red dress would be perfect with your dark hair. Mrs. Lynn is never wrong when it comes to these things ya know. Having four grown daughters me-self, I have done tons of mending, matching, and buying of dresses."

I chuckled. "Thank you, Mrs. Lynn, you are too kind. You are right, the red does look lovely." I twirled around, admiring the dress and how it flowed. It felt like a dream. Its sleek design was so different from the layers upon layers I usually wore. It was breathable but still beautiful. It would be hard to go back to the squeezing corsets and mounds of fabric once I left this place.

"Here is a cloak, since these lands are a bit chilly this time of year." Looking up, she was holding it out to me. I came forward as she helped me slip it around my shoulders and fussed with the top three buttons that kept it in place. It felt good to be pampered again. It reminded me of my old handmaiden, Trinity, and the great care she gave to me for years before mother dismissed her. She was just as sweet as Mrs. Lynn, and I held back tears as I remembered how she would fuss over me too.

"There, deary, I think we are ready to head out now." Then she patted my arm and went to a chair by the fireplace, grabbing a shawl and placing it around her shoulders. It was so thin compared to the cloak I was wearing. I stepped towards her, worried.

"Mrs. Lynn, Won't you catch a chill with that thin shawl?" After all she had done for me, I could not let her catch a cold if it was as chilly as she said it was.

"Aren't you a dear, but don't you fuss about old Mrs. Lynn. I am used to these lands, and this here shawl will do me just fine. If it gets too cold, I'll bring us right back in." Then she patted my hand and linked her arm in mine, and we headed out the door into the hallway.

The hall was long and surprisingly very well lit. The natural light was provided by tall windows that were placed on the left side, between every two doors or so. They were not stained with color, but intricate designs of flowers and trees were what formed the clear glass. When I found out I was in the dark fae lands, I expected dreary hallways with cobwebs and chains hanging everywhere to let their guests know they have come to their doom. Instead, I was greeted with beautiful designs and structures that almost seemed magical. I looked to the right and tapestries of stunning gardens and paintings depicting fae, who were playing instruments as animals gathered around to listen.

I was captivated by this enchanting place. I was also confused since the man who owned this keep did not conform to the surroundings that now encircled me. Maybe I was wrong, and what Mrs. Lynn told me about his highness was true. While I didn't believe it at the time for some reason, I believed it now. The truth settled deep in my heart, and it was as if a burden had lifted off of my shoulders. My mind and my heart were now in agreement. It felt strange, but I could not deny it. If he was not the culprit responsible for their deaths. Then who was? I know my mother was involved, but who else agreed to help her if not him? Was it the King of these dark lands? Did he have a close resemblance to the prince?

I continued to contemplate the events in my mind and what I did know about him, which was not much. Maybe there was a misunderstanding, some loophole I was missing. No matter how much it made sense that he was the one who helped my mother, the strong feeling of his innocence outweighed any other notion.

The stories Mrs. Lynn has been telling me the last few days only proved his character to be honorable. He treated those in his care with dignity and respect. He also has taken extra steps to ensure my own comfort. It would have been so easy to just have left me in the woods after I fainted to finish what he started with my family all those years ago. Yet he brought me back here to be taken care of and offered me not only a comfortable room, but an endearing companion. There was more to this man than meets the eye, and I was determined to have this mysterious fae solved by the time I left here. I would make sure of it, because I really wanted to know who this dark fae prince really was.

As we continued to make our way down the hall, I noticed that flowers started to appear just outside the great windows. I recognized roses, daisies, and vines that started to crawl along the trim on the outside. We reached the door at the end of the hall and I hoped it led into the beautiful greenery that I was seeing through the glass panes.

I realized Mrs. Lynn was still chatting away, but I was too distracted by my thoughts and the magnificent scenery before me that I did not catch what she was saying. Hoping she didn't realize I was lost in thought, I tuned in as she opened the door before us, leading into a glass house.

"Now, these gardens have not been taken care of as they should, but they still provide some color to this place. As I was saying, Her Majesty, bless her soul, when she was young and married to our former king, she would come here and tend to the flowers when they came to visit Grauntrea."

She continued speaking about the former queen, but I was mesmerized by all the different flowers and plants that were running wild with growth throughout the small dome-shaped sanctuary. Vibrant colors of blue, purple, yellow, pink, and red were mixed in. No order to their arrangement as far as I could tell. The sun was peeking through the glass that brought a sparkle to the air giving it an enchanting look. I never wanted to leave.

She tugged me to the right, and I followed down the stone path. Trying to catch all the different types of flowers that I had never seen before, wondering if they were native to this land or cross-breeds that the queen grew. Maybe Mrs. Lynn already mentioned what they were, but I wasn't paying attention like I should, so I didn't dare ask her for fear of being caught in my negligence to her words.

We made it to the end of the greenhouse and went through another arched door. I was sad to leave this enchanted place behind but grateful it was so close to the quarters I was currently staying in. I would come back later, I told myself.

We entered the outer gardens, but they were not as vibrant as the ones inside, but at least the fresh air filled my lungs. It was a little chilly like Mrs. Lynn said it would be, but the sun was still out and shining, bringing warmth to my face through the chill. It felt so good that I stopped and basked in its sensation, closing my eyes as I tilted my face towards warmth.

"Ah, seems to be a good day, hopefully the sun will stay shining, and we can enjoy the rest of our walk before it starts to rain."

I opened my eyes, seeing the clear, blue skies and confusion pulled at my brow.

"Rain?"

"Oh, yes. These old bones start to ache when I feel a storm coming on. It may not look like it now, but I have never been wrong. Nope, not ever. You just trust Mrs. Lynn when she says there is a storm a brewing.

I smiled down at her, guessing I better enjoy the sun while it lasts, since I have already been cooped up for almost a week now. Whether her bones told the truth of the rain or not, I did not want to waste time finding out.

"Well, Mrs. Lynn, you just lead the way and I'll follow."

She led me through the stone pathway, talking about all the different flowers and the history of the castle. Most of it was full of hardship and how most of the humans and fae were in bondage to their king in some form or the other.

"But not here. No, the prince won't do that to us. He refused to have blood bonds with anyone in his service."

"Blood bond? What is that?" It sounded frightening.

"Oh, don't you worry your little head over it, dear. The prince would never bond you to him. I used to be bonded to the queen until she died. Only way to break a bond ye see. She always treated me with kindness though. I was blessed I tell you, so very blessed. Many fae and humans are treated with less dignity and respect, but not I. "

She tsked and continued to lead me through the gardens. I was still curious about this bond?

"What happens to those who are bonded?" I asked her.

"Well, the king likes having humans as servants, 'scum only good for labor,' he calls them. So, he would steal the poor dears away from nearby villages, but your kind lifespans are so short that he was tired of constantly finding replacements. So, he created a blood bond that allowed them to share the life force with him and live an eternal life of servitude." I gasped at her shocking words. Maybe I didn't need the answers I sought, just a way out of this place.

"Oh, yes, a lifetime bonded to the one who cast the bond."

"Is there actual blood involved?" I asked warily, not really wanting to know the answer, but my curiosity got the better of me.

"Sadly, yes." She answered quietly, looking down at her hands. This was the first time I have seen her anything but cheerful and my heart reached out to her. I gave her arm that was linked to mine a gentle squeeze.

"But don't dwell on such thoughts dear, you are safe here." She patted my hand assuring me.

I know she just said I had nothing to worry about with the prince, but I was still in the Kingdom of a King who created such bonds. The thought of being in servitude to a malicious ruler for the rest of my days made me anxious and a shiver of fear went through my body.

We continued through the winding paths and the closer we got to the gardens exit the sounds of clashing metal pierced my ears. I looked to Mrs. Lynn to see if we should be worried but she seemed as if nothing was out of place. Then we stepped through and I saw a training yard in front of me and my worries eased. It was full of fae soldiers training in leather vests that buttoned up to their neck. It was the tall dark fae with black hair that curled at the ends that captured my attention.

The prince was quick as he spared not only one, but two men. He held a sword in his right hand and a large dagger in the other. He moved with grace as he dodged and struck at his opponents. Sweat was glistening down his face as he stepped back to dodge a blow to his chest. He turned and ducked under the shorter of the two opponents, knocking his sword from his hand as he went. This caused the fae to falter, which allowed the prince to quickly come around to his back and hook him around the neck with such speed that I almost missed the maneuver. He placed his dagger at his opponent's throat and his sword pointing at the other guard. His opponent yielded by putting his hands up, and they both dropped their swords to their side, breathing heavily from the training. He dropped his dagger and let the man go from his grasp. A smile that reached his eyes and lit up his face as laughter spilled from their lips. They slapped each other's backs in friendly sportsmanship.

Butterflies filled my stomach as his laughter reached my ears. I could not look away from this magnificent fae before me. He was so different from the man in the woods. So carefree and relaxed. I was drawn to him in a way that I did not understand.

Suddenly, his head turned in my direction, and his eyes locked on mine.

I could not look away. His eyebrows pulled together, and his men turned to see what made their leader's conduct change. I quickly looked down, breaking our connection as my whole body filled with embarrassment. I hastily scanned the gardens, looking for Mrs. Lynn, anything to get me away from their scrutiny. I was surprised to see that she turned around and was heading back to the greenhouse without me.

I could feel the pressure of his gaze still on me, and I dared to look up before following Mrs. Lynn back inside. The scowl was replaced with a questioning look, and I flushed even further at his inquiry. He no doubt was wondering why I was here and I wondered the same thing.

I quickly curtsied and turned to catch up with Mrs. Lynn, who was far down the path.

Chapter 16

DEVRON

"Great work, Joel. You *almost* had me." I smirked and laughed at the guard I was training with, who was currently being held by a dagger placed on his neck. He scoffed as I released him and slapped him playfully on the back. They joined in with my laughter.

"It's good to see you this way, Your Highness, it's been too long," Marrin said, my other component in our friendly bout.

It was then I could sense her stare. I looked towards the garden entrance, and my eyes locked onto hers, and heat filled my chest. Her figure was framed by the hedge, and she looked radiant in her garnet-colored dress, her cheeks growing to a similar color. I raised my brows in humor as she realized I caught her observing me. I could tell she was frantically looking for an escape. I looked around for Mrs. Lynn, who should have been close by. I gave her orders not to let Helen roam free since it wasn't safe. Not when my brother was already down my throat. I noticed a gray head bobbing its way back to the greenhouse, and relief came when she turned to make her way back to my old nursemaid.

"Is that the girl from Retna, the one you brought back?" Marrin asked, amused. Looking at him, then around the training yard, I realized some of my men had stopped their sparring and were staring at me with smug looks on their faces.

"Yes," I answered indifferently. What I was about to do would not help my situation with the girl who just disappeared into the garden. I did not care though, I had to speak with her. My men could just keep their thoughts to themselves.

"Continue your practice. I'll be right back," I told them sternly.

A few of them chuckled as I leaped over the low wooden posts that encircled the training yard, but I ignored them. Making my way into the garden entrance, I saw her opening the door to my mother's conservatory and rushed after her.

Chapter 17

HELEN

I rushed through the garden, embarrassed the prince and his men saw me gawking at him. I had to get away and find Mrs. Lynn as fast as possible. I was struggling to breathe since my energy was still low from fighting a fever for so many days. I was almost to the door when he called out to me.

"Lady Helen! A moment please!"

How did he know my name? I don't recall ever telling it to him. It dawned on me that he probably found out from Mrs. Lynn. Who knows what information I gave her while I was delusional with fever. It felt like so much had happened in the last couple of weeks since the festival in Retna. Here

I was in the dark fae lands. Prisoner or guest to this prince? I still was not sure. Now, the same man was chasing me down through the gardens. I stopped and slowly turned to meet him.

"Yes, Your Highness?" I asked softly, dipping into a curtsey. Wondering what he wanted with me, hoping he would let me go and not keep me here at his castle once I found out all of the answers to my questions first.

He stopped a few feet in front of me with his hands on his hips, catching his breath, no doubt from sparring with his men and then chasing me down.

I looked up at his tall frame that towered over me, my head just barely reaching his chin. His dark waves glistening from his exercise, and his muscles showing proof that he trained regularly. He had a smirk on his face as his eyes locked onto mine. My body reacted again as I looked back into his dark gray eyes. It was the first time I've seen them up close, since every other time he was wearing a hooded cloak. They reminded me of skies when it thundered and rained, dark and powerful, just like he was. Heat of a different kind took over my cheeks, and butterflies swarmed my stomach. Not liking the reaction I was having to him I stood up straighter with my head held high, raising my eyebrows. His smirk only grew, and a chuckle escaped. He stepped closer to me, and I only raised my head higher in defiance. Royalty or not, he had the answers that I needed.

"Do you like what you see?" He winked, putting his arms out to the side, displaying his perfectly toned body. The nerve of this man!

"Hmph! No!" I turned on my heel and continued to make my way through the gardens, far away from this infuriating man. Berating myself on getting caught gawking at this man before me, not only once, but twice in less than five minutes. I could hear the clicking of his heels right behind me on the stone pathway. I rushed and finally made it to the far end of the greenhouse and reached out to the handle to twist it open. A hand came over my shoulder and pressed against the door, preventing me from opening it. Quickly turning back around I realized I was now trapped between the door and this man as he placed his other hand next to my head. I tilted my head back to look up at my captor, keeping the fear from my eyes. His eyes were intense, as if a storm itself was taking place within. He searched my face with longing, and my breath caught. My fear went away and was replaced with the emotion to match his. His vision traveled down to my lips and back to my eyes. My own gaze following suit. He leaned forward slightly, and my heart pounded. Waiting. Anticipating. Closing my eyes, my feet started to lift to close the gap between us.

I felt him step away from me, and I opened my eyes and found he was facing away from me. Embarrassment overcame me, then anger, followed by disappointment. I felt like a fool! Did I want him to kiss me? Breathing in deeply to clear my mind and get ahold of myself and these frightening feelings. I could not grow attached to this man I barely knew. Especially, with the reasons I had.

A frustrated groan escaped him as he ran his hand through his hair. Did he regret being so close to me? After a few moments of watching him, which also allowed me to gather myself, he finally broke the tense silence between us.

He cleared his throat. "It seems like you are feeling better?" he asked in a thick voice. His hands, now hanging by his sides, gave him a look of defeat.

The urge to reach out and comfort him was overwhelming, but I stayed where I was. It was easier to talk to him without the distraction of his mesmerizing eyes and features taunting me, especially after what had almost just happened between us. I swallowed, trying to find my voice.

"I am, thank you," I replied softly.

"And Mrs. Lynn? Is she suitable for your needs?"

"Yes, she has gone above and beyond in making sure my every need is met."

He nodded once. "Good."

Wondering if I should ask him all the questions in my mind since it was easier to talk to him with his back turned to me, I took a deep breath and prayed for the best as I stepped towards him, the words spilling from my lips. Desperation for answers overcoming any embarrassment I previously had.

"Why am I here?" I softly pleaded. "I'm not sure what I have to offer you. I know you said you weren't involved with my aunt and uncle. For some odd reason, I believe you. What happened to them? I have so many questions."

He slightly turned and looked at me, catching my gaze. A worried expression overcame him. I looked down at my feet, avoiding his gaze. It was easier this way to get it all out.

"Why bargain for me? Am I in danger? What have you done with my mother?"

Silence continued as he looked to the ceiling, then shook his head, letting out a breath.

"So many questions, but I guess you deserve the answers."

I eagerly awaited.

"Your mother is where she should be. I sent her with my guards to the constable in your little town, to pay for her deeds against your family. While I did not kill your aunt and uncle, I was involved."

"Involved? How?" Anger resurfaced. Maybe I was wrong about him.

"I don't have the answers just yet, but I am working on finding them."

"Finding them? They're dead!" I cried at him, my emotions overcoming me again.

"They're not, actually."

My breath caught, and my heart pounded. They were alive? It was not possible.

"Explain. I don't understand." How could they be alive when their gravestones were in the cemetery outside our little town?

"My second in command, Nor, hid them away from your mother, and used a transformation spell on a dying couple in your town to look like them. We knew she was determined to kill them, so we had to make it believable. I swear, no harm came to them."

A transformation spell?

"The same you used on me?"

"Yes." Then he looked at me with sorrow in his eyes, stepping towards me. I stepped back, afraid. He paused, a sad smile forming his lips. "I'm sorry for what I did. I had no right to use you in that way, but I could not let your mother hurt you if we did not go along with her ploy. I had to think of a way to get you out of her grasp while still holding her accountable. Transforming you gave me time."

"You tricked me, though!" I said half-heartedly.

I could not be fully mad at him when he thought his actions were somewhat noble. Maybe I was too forgiving. Then, I thought over the past five years that I needed to be forgiven of as well. How I treated my cousin and the hardship she had to suffer because of it. I had to fix this. Maybe, we both needed forgiveness in our lives. While I did not agree with how he handled it, he did save me from my mother's madness. Why was this whole situation so twisted? Why did so many lives have to be upturned and torn because of one woman's cruel intentions?

"Why haven't they come back? Surely, they would not want to be away from their daughter?"

"We did not know they had a daughter at the time. He searched the house after they returned to make sure no other members of the family were there, but it was only them. He erased their memory to forget where they came from and placed them in a new kingdom to start over."

I thought back on that night of the festival and realized Claira stayed at my house to sleep. We had just lost Lillian and we were grieving our friend.

Erased their memory? They will never know Claira, me, or anyone ever again? Tears choked me and I barely got out my question. "Can it be undone?"

"I don't know." It was so much to process that I did not realize he stepped in front of me again, until he grabbed my hands and brought them to his chest. My heart pounding out of mine. He searched my eyes once more, his own looked as if a battle raged behind his dark lashes.

"But I will try my hardest to make it right. My commander is looking for them now."

Then dropping my hands, he turned on his heel and walked back out into the open gardens. So many emotions were running through me as I watched him walk away. Hope, forgiveness, relief, and something else I could not quite name.

I went back to my room when I could no longer see him. I had much to think about. As I headed down the hallway thunder sounded outside and a smile came to my face, Mrs. Lynn was right; a storm was brewing.

Once I made it back to my room I put my cloak away and started to pace. My mind tried to take in everything that was said between me and the prince. I could not believe it, my aunt and uncle were alive and someone was searching for them now. The relief that they were alive was overwhelming and I could only think of my cousin and how the news would bring such joy to her life.

The door opened, and hope rose in my chest only to be filled with slight disappointment. It was Mrs. Lynn carrying a tray. While I didn't mind it was her, I was just hoping she was someone else. Someone whose eyes matched the storm outside.

"Sorry to leave you, deary, I could feel the storm brewing and decided to make us a nice cup of herbal tea to wait it out. It is sunflower, too! The best remedy for gray skies if you ask me. Oh, but let us not waste time talking about it. Drink it while it is hot. Now, that's a dear."

I took the cup from her hands and sipped the refreshing liquid. It was delicious. She was right, it was just what we needed. We chatted about the gardens and my thoughts drifted to the prince as we ate sweetcakes with our tea.

"Ah, now that our bellies are full, shall we take a tour my dear? Can't have you losing your way around here. With so many rooms and endless halls one is bound to get lost without the correct guidance."

"That sounds wonderful, Mrs. Lynn. I'd be honored to tour the keep." I was excited to learn more about the man who ruled this keep and whose opinion I had of was drastically changing for the better.

"Right this way, deary, right this way. Mrs. Lynn will make sure you know where everything is."

We went out into the hallway that was brightly lit with candles. The only explanation could be that they were enhanced my magic since there were no shadows to be found.

After a few turns, we ended up in front of a large set of wooden doors that were slightly ajar.

"This here is the library. His Highness has quite the collection. When he was younger, he would have me read to him every night. Only way the boy would sleep, I tell you. Those were the days. Now he is all grown up and running his keep, too busy for such things anymore."

We stepped into the large room, filled with books from the floor to the ceiling. Shelves scattered around the room to hold what the walls could not. Chairs and couches were placed before a large fire, beckoning me to come, sit, and read for a while.

"Now, let us move on to the portrait gallery. This way, deary, this way." She hustled me out of the room. I told myself I would return later this evening when the house was settled and I wouldn't disturb anyone.

We again made our way down to the hall and turned into a large room that was filled with paintings. Portraits of fae were everywhere, along with depictions of war, some of which made my heart sink as humans were depicted as slaves. One particular painting at the end of the gallery caught my attention above the rest. It was of a family;

mother, father, and three children. Two boys and a little girl, whose long black curls and vibrant gray eyes matched that of the mild child's features. I would know those eyes anywhere…it was the prince. I looked back at the little girl. He had a sister? I wonder where she was? Then my gaze drifted to the oldest boy, who had straight black hair and wore a thin circlet, no doubt representing the heir. He looked just like the man, who stood next to a beautiful woman, with long soft curls that flowed to her waist.

I focused on the girl and the younger boy. He looked so sad, and my heart reached out to him. He never mentioned a sister, though. Not that we talked much about family matters. The only words we have exchanged so far were the answering of my questions, and those were close to heated conversations, nothing cordial.

"Ah, it seems you have found the family portrait." I turned to see Mrs. Lynn come up next to me as she examined the painting with pursed lips.

Maybe she would tell me why the prince was so sad and who his sister was. I watched her, eagerly awaiting her to spill information she has so far been free to give. I noticed her eyes glistening as she touched the young girl in the portrait. I reached out and touched her arm to offer her comfort. She must have cared deeply for the girl.

"His Highness was so young…" Her head sank as she turned and headed back towards the door "tis not my story to tell, though." My curiosity burned within me and I was disappointed she didn't freely give me more information.

"Come deary, there is much to see."

I glanced one more time at the portrait before following her to finish the tour of the castle.

I barely paid attention to the rest of the tour, and she soon led me back to my rooms.

"Thank you for the tour, Mrs. Lynn. It was good to become more familiar with my surroundings. The castle is beautiful."

"Oh, what a sweet thing you are. Yes, his highness tries to take care of his keep and gives many of the townsfolk work to keep it that way. A fair wage too, if there ever was one. Now sit tight, and I'll be back with some hot supper for you. I'm hoping it's soup, just the thing for this storm since it fills the belly mighty good."

While she was gone, I put away my cloak and looked around my room. Running my hand over the furniture and the high-quality material it was made of, pondering how we once had such fine things. Making my way to the desk I opened the center drawer and found paper, an ink bottle, and a quill to write with. I would write to my cousin once Prince Devron's commander came back with word about my aunt and uncle. In the meantime, I could get to know this mysterious prince and his past that seemed to trouble him, like the boy in the painting. There was more to his handsome fae than he let on, and I wanted to know more. I decided that instead of the library, I would go back there tonight and study this family portrait. Thunder boomed outside as I paced my room, waiting for Mrs. Lynn, my thoughts on those gray eyes that matched the weather outside.

Chapter 18

DEVRON

I was torn at leaving her in the conservatory, but I had to get away. Not only from her presence that was drawing me in the longer I stayed there, but the memories the glass dome gave me. It was my mother's sanctuary when she would visit Grauntrea.

Once I got past the gardens, I headed towards the stables and had Attono, my large black stallion, saddled. Riding towards the forest pathway I heard thunder in the distance and looked up to see gray skies rolling in from the west. My determination to get away only grew, hoping the storm would soothe my thoughts and nerves.

"Ya!" I shouted, nudging the large stallion with my heels, urging him into a gallop. Heading into the forest's path, we dodged trees and jumped over rotting wood that spread across the forest floor. The wind and cool air whipped the hair from my face as I pressed Attono for speed. Both our hearts beat rapidly as we raced across the wooded lands until we finally came to the edge of an open meadow. I pulled on the reins, slowing him down to a trot. Looking up to see the gray skies have almost caught up to us. Lightning struck down in the distance, and I once again pushed Attono until we raced across the meadow, the wind whipping through my hair once more, as my heart finally lifted. The burdens seemed to float away as we flew across the even ground. Each pounding step of my stallion's hooves pushed down the heartache and pain.

This is what it felt like to be free. Free of pain. Free of regret.

Drops of water started to splash on my face, and I slowed Attono down. We were both breathing hard from our invigorating ride.

"Good boy," I told him while patting his neck, then turned him around to head back to our keep. I didn't push him this time as we trotted across the meadow once more and into the forest. The trees left just enough of an opening to allow the rain to soak through my hair and tunic. I didn't care because right now, my worries were being washed away as the water dripped down me. Grateful that the large beast I was riding seemed to understand my need for this short felt peace.

The storm was in full force when we finally made it back to the stables. I told my stable groom I would take care of his needs and brushed him until his coat was dry. Then fed him the muchdeserved oats and grains from a large bucket.

Once I finally left the stables, I headed back inside. Taking off my drenched tunic, hoping to free my scars from the pull of the wet cloth, I made my way to the portrait gallery. It seemed my sense of peace would only last so long as the storm raged outside and within my heart.

I pushed open the doors and headed straight to the family portrait. The large fire in the hearth gave light to the colors on the painting before me. Looking at the little girl in the picture, regret came over me. Andrea, my sister, was so young when the accident happened. It was all my fault, too. I was so new to my powers, and my father was in a rage that day.

I rolled back my shoulders as the scars pulled, constantly reminding me of the whippings he bestowed upon me on that stormy night. While fae could heal, I was still learning at the time they were given, being so young and vulnerable. The wounds were so deep that they scarred, and not just my flesh; there were scars that no one could see.

Suddenly, I could feel her presence. She was just outside the doorway of the gallery. Panic rose at her learning about my past and that it would ruin all the progress I have made in trying to redeem myself. Hoping she was heading to the library and would not see me as she walked by. My false optimism was shattered when a gasp came from the doorway, no doubt from the horror of the scars on my skin.

Chapter 19

HELEN

Making my way down the hall toward the gallery with a candle in my hand lighting my way. I was eager to reach my destination. I turned the corner to an already opened door. My breath caught as I saw the prince standing in front of the family portrait I came to study. Then my cheeks filled with heat realizing he was shirtless. I should have stepped out immediately, but my gaze noticed the thick red scars all across his back. No doubt from a whip. A gasp escaped my lips on its own accord as I looked over the marks, my heart sinking. Who did such a vile thing to him? His shoulders sank, his head bowed, and I realized he must have heard me. Tears filled my eyes as I stepped back into the hallway, ready to escape what I just saw.

"Don't go." He spoke softly which made me turn back towards him. It was the desperation in his voice that made me stop. I hesitated at first, then my feet slowly moved across the gallery, stopping a few feet from him and the pain he must have endured permanently etched onto his skin.

I hesitated, but curiosity got the better of me as I traced one of the scars along his back. The jagged skin under my fingers told a story of suffering. He tensed, and I withdrew immediately, hoping I didn't offend him.

"What happened?" I softly asked."

"It was a long time ago. A mistake I hope never to repeat again."

A mistake? What could possibly have happened to make a young prince endure this?

"Who did this to you?

He breathed in and turned, looking straight into my eyes, which I made sure to keep my own on, with how he was displayed before me. My cheeks burned with embarrassment at catching him in such a state.

"My father got into a rage when I was younger and decided to punish me for my inability to fulfill my role as his second son. My sister," He paused and turned to look at the young girl in the portrait "came running to save me from my father's wrath when I lost control of my powers, and I accidentally…" He hung his head low. Tears now streamed down my cheeks as the sound of thunder filled the room, echoing in the gallery. His heartache was louder, though and it pierced my soul.

"These scars serve as a reminder of that day." He turned to me; his eyes filled with agony. I stepped forward and wrapped my arms around him pulling him close, showing him that I cared. I was surprised when he willingly returned the embrace in a tight hold, his hands wrapping around my waist as if I was the only thing that kept him from drowning in this cruel world. Then he abruptly let go of me and turned back to the portrait. I missed being in his arms already and longed for another embrace.

"You should go, this place holds no happy thoughts or memories."

I nodded, realizing he needed time to himself. Turning to leave, I only walked a few steps before he called back to me.

"Lady Helen?" I turned back to meet his gaze, which was full of longing.

"Yes, Your Highness?"

"Please, call me Devron."

Hesitating at first since it would put us on a more personal level, but deep down, I knew I wanted that connection with him, even if it amounted to nothing. We have already shared so much in our short amount of time, it seemed fitting.

"Yes…Devron." A tingle went through me when speaking his name. "I offer you the same courtesy."

He nodded.

"Thank you, Helen." My heart soared at hearing the familiarity of my name on his lips. Then a smile tugged at his lips.

"Tomorrow, would you like to come with me to tour my keep?"

"That would be wonderful." I curtsied, then rushed out of the gallery, anticipating what tomorrow would bring.

Chapter 20

DEVRON

I made my way back to my room and thought about how she reacted to me. Relief that I felt sympathy instead of disgust as she touched the scarred tissue across my back made me spill the tale of how I got them, even though it left me vulnerable. Something I hated feeling, but her presence made me feel safe in that moment.

Then, when she wrapped her arms around me, it was as if she was the only thing keeping me together. Something I haven't felt for so long, except with Nor, Mrs. Lynn and my men. They knew my story, though. She did not. I hated letting her go, but I forced myself to pull back from our embrace due to propriety, kicking myself that I did not put on another tunic before I made my way to the gallery.

Not wanting our time to end, I quickly thought of a way I could interact with her that didn't always involve us constantly meeting by chance. Touring my keep seemed the best way. It was out in the open, and she could see how I treated my people. That I was different from my brother and father. The desire to prove myself to her was undeniable, even though it might not lead to anything since she couldn't stay here. I knew that, but Nor still hadn't returned with the answers about her aunt and uncle, so I still had some time, and I wouldn't waste it. My heart yearned for more time and ached for something that could never be.

The thunder still sounded outside as lightning struck, lighting my room, but the storm outside was nothing compared to the one inside my heart.

Chapter 21

HELEN

I woke up early, anticipating the day. Mrs. Lynn came hustling in as usual with the breakfast tray.

"Today should be a fine day, it seems. No ache in my bones, but nothing a good strong ginger tea can't fix if that were the case. Here I am blathering again. We need to get you ready; the prince is waiting." It seems Devron told Mrs. Lynn of our plans this morning, for which I was grateful. While I trusted the prince, I was still in dark fae lands, ruled by this ruthless brother. It was comforting to know that she knew where we would be, just in case.

"Are you sure, Mrs. Lynn? I can dress myself." Not wanting to cause her more discomfort than the weather already did. It was not a problem since I'd already been dressing myself for years. Ever since my mother let the household go I made sure to buy dresses that could be done up in the front to make it easier on myself.

"Oh, no. Don't put me to shame, deary. I'm fit as a fiddle. What would the prince think of me neglecting my duties to you. You just eat up while I get your riding habit ready."

"Riding?"

"Oh, yes, how else did you think to see Grauntrea? Walking on foot would take all day, and what a fine day it will be."

"But I've never ridden before." I panicked.

"Oh, well, I'm sure his highness will think of something. Now, don't look so distressed. He won't let anything happen to you. Now, hurry and eat up, dear. The day is young, and we must get you dressed. We can't have the prince waiting and thinking we've been dawdling, now can we?"

I lost my appetite but obeyed her nonetheless. Riding couldn't be that hard, could it? It is not that I wasn't around horses, it's just I've always walked or have been pulled in a carriage. Father was the one who rode when he had to go out of town for business.

Not wanting to let this little fear prevent me from spending time with the Devron, I became determined to try. Praying I would not make a fool of myself in the meantime.

After helping me into a gown that had more layers and cloth than normal fae attire, she led me out to the stables.

Devron and two of his men, the ones he was sparring with yesterday, were standing by their horses waiting for me. Making my way towards them, Devron came up to me and offered me a hand, sending tingles along my arm. Looking at our clasped fingers, I made my way up to his mouth where a broad smile was in place just for me.

Wondering what it would be like to kiss those tempting lips. I blinked, clearing my thoughts as I looked at his eyes, not helping my resolve as his gaze drifted down to my own mouth. I needed to be careful with this man, else I'll lose my heart completely.

"My lady, do you ride?" bringing my attention to a tan-colored mare that was next to a large black stallion. I hesitated, my hands twisting with fear, hoping he didn't think me incompetent when I told him no. I also noticed we were back to formalities. It made sense since we were in front of his men, but I missed the familiarity we reached with one another.

"I have not ridden before, no, but I am willing to learn your highness." I swallowed, pushing down my fear.

He stepped closer to me and looked down at my shaking hands. He grabbed them and brought them to his chest. My fear instantly left and was immediately replaced with something else.

“It’s Devron, my lady.” He whispered, sending chills down my spine. I hesitated, then looked towards his men and back to him, noticing they both had wide grins in place as they stared ahead, trying to give us a sense of privacy. He followed my gaze, and disappointment settled on his features when he realized my predicament. He mumbled something I didn’t quite hear, then instead of leading me to the light mare, he brought me to his black stallion.

“This is Attono, he is gentle and fierce, just like his name. If you are okay with it, you could ride with me?”

Knowing I would be so close to him, and it was sure to make a statement, but I would at least be safer than if I rode by myself since I had no previous riding experience. Nodding my agreement, he led me around to the tall stallion, who patiently waited. I looked around, seeing how I could get up in the saddle, when suddenly a squeal left my lips as Devron grabbed me by the waist and lifted me up onto the saddle with my feet hanging over the edge.

I quickly grabbed the horn to balance myself as he swung up behind me, placing my back right up against his chest. It made my whole body flush and I leaned forward trying to give us some space.

"You're going to fall off my lady if you lean any farther," he teased as he whispered in my ear, sending tingles down my neck. "I wouldn't want my men to think I shoved you off my horse, what kind of prince would that make me."

I turned in the saddle to rebuke him, only to stop since his mouth was now so close to mine. I immediately turned back to the front, forgetting the rebuttal, only aware of how close we were and the heat that burned my cheeks.

A chuckle escaped him and I didn't dare look to see how his men were reacting to our interaction. He reached around me and pulled me closer to him, enclosing me in his arms as he grabbed the reins and we started our journey towards Grauntrea. I breathed in deeply, hoping he couldn't feel or hear my pounding heart. I should have taken a chance with the mare since we would be this close for the whole day.

"Breath Helen, it's just a horse." He whispered the assurance in my ear that didn't help get air into my lungs at all, in fact, he took it away.

"It's not the horse Devron, it's…" I couldn't finish my sentence. I didn't want him to know I was greatly affected by his close presence. He chuckled, and I instantly knew he understood my predicament. I stiffened in his arms.

"Helen, there is no place I would rather have you be than right here in my arms. Fate has blessed me with this. Relax."

I nodded and took another deep breath, and settled against his chest again. Glad that was where he wanted me to be since I felt the same way.

We entered the town just outside the keep and found it busy with fae. It reminded me of Retna, except their beauty outshined those of our human race, along with their attire. The buildings seemed the same, and everyone we passed was friendly as they greeted their prince, along with shock as they studied the young maiden he was holding as we rode through town. He explained to me how he came to rule this area. His mother's father was Lord, and they inherited it when she married his father.

"My brother let me have jurisdiction over the Keep once he became king."

We talked about his brother, and I remembered Mrs. Lynn talking about how the king blood bonded humans and fae to him. While she told me Devron would never do that, I needed to satiate my need to know if it was true.

"Mrs. Lynn talked about a blood bond. Are any of them blood-bonded to you?"

He stiffened in his saddle, and I immediately regretted my words, knowing I should not have asked.

"No," he stated, sounding hurt that I would accuse him of such a thing. "I am not my brother. Everyone here is free."

Relief overcame me along with guilt, afraid I just ruined what little connection we had made with each other. I touched his arm that wrapped around me and turned in the saddle, realizing I needed to apologize. We were so close and it took me a few seconds to gather my thoughts.

"I am sorry. I did not mean to accuse you of such a thing. I know you are not your brother. I can see that now. Please forgive me." I softly pleaded to him, looking into his eyes, hoping he saw that I meant it.

Then his fingers were in my hair as he gently brushed them to the back of my neck, his eyes searching mine. Then cupping my face, he leaned towards me and gently pressed his soft lips to mine. It was perfect and I returned the kiss with eagerness, only to quickly realize we were still riding down the middle of the town. I broke our kiss, hearing chuckles from his men, and faced forward, my face burning with heat at our embrace.

I could hear him sigh behind me.

"I am sorry for my harsh tone Helen, I know you don't think of me like that, and for..." Not wanting him to think I regretted kissing him, just the circumstance. I turned once again in the saddle, surprised at my boldness and bravery, I gave him a small smile and quickly kissed him on the lips to show him there was nothing to be sorry for. A broad smile replaced his warry one and I leaned against his chest a breath of relief escaping both of us. Grateful the tension was broken as he continued telling me about his keep and the fae who dwelled here. Not knowing where this would lead since he was royalty, and I was just a girl from a small town. I pushed those worries aside and decided to enjoy the moment with him. We stopped at a bakery and ate a delectable treat while his men stood outside the shop guarding us. As we continued talking to those in the village, I noticed this dark fae prince was loved and respected by all we encountered. About midday, we headed back to the keep, my thoughts on the prince whose arms I was in. He was so different from the man I met two weeks ago, and if I was honest, so was I. These thoughts brought me back to Claira.

He helped me down, then gently grabbed my chin with his finger and tilted it up to look at him. His eyes searching mine.

"Are you okay? Did you not enjoy yourself today?"

"I did immensely. Thank you, Devron, for everything."

"What's wrong?"

I sighed, realizing I needed to share the truth with him as well, since he openly entrusted me with his. That I also need redemption.

"I need to tell you something." Then I hesitated. He grabbed my hand and turned towards his men giving them instruction, then led me back into the keep and to the library. Once we were settled on a settee he turned to me, grabbing my hands.

"What is it, love? You can tell me anything."

My heart fluttered at his endearment. Did he really feel that way? It gave me the courage I needed to be vulnerable with him. Starting my story, I told him about my cousin and I. How I treated her over the years, due to fear and my mother's manipulating ways, but that I was still guilty since I had a choice on how I should have treated her.

He reached up and wiped my tears with his thumbs that were streaming down my face. He pulled me to his chest and held me for a while. Feeling the security and comfort that I did not realize I needed.

He pressed his lips to my forehead and whispered, "Everyone has done things in their life they will regret. It is what we do in the now, to make up for our actions, that determines our worth, even if they are not here to see it." Knowing he was talking about his sister and his own redemption gave me hope for my own, but Claira was still alive and I wanted to have her forgiveness.

"I don't know if I can be redeemed for what I have done. How could I ever make it up to her? She is with the fae king."

He placed his hands on my cheeks and lifted them up to meet his determined gaze. "While my cousin and I are not on good terms, I promise you that once my commander comes back with information about your aunt and uncle, I will take you to his kingdom myself so that you can speak with your cousin."

I nodded and leaned once again on his chest. He held me as our broken hearts started to heal as hope took place in them.

Chapter 22

DEVRON

She fell asleep in my arms and love bloomed inside my chest for this girl who let herself be so vulnerable with me. I could not deny the feeling that coursed through my body. I wanted to make her mine, to have her rule this little keep with me. I've never wanted anything so badly as I looked at her dark lashes splayed against her cheeks and her pink lips so tempting.

I picked her up, carried her to her room, and immediately left, letting Mrs. Lynn know we were back and that Helen was asleep in her room.

Then making my way to the throne room, I sat down on my seat as I mulled over what could be done about Helen and these strong feelings I felt towards her. Knowing I could not keep her here brought an ache in my heart that was overwhelming, the thought of losing her made me catch my breath. She had to leave with my brother reigning; he would eventually find out about her, and he would take her away from me. Power surged to my fingers and whipped around my hands at the thought of him touching her. I would never allow that to happen.

Why couldn't I be like my light fae cousin? Who not only found his bride but could keep her as well. For the first time in my life, envy for King Leon coursed through my veins. I have never once been jealous of him, but the dark-haired beauty now asleep in her room made me wish more than ever that I was him.

Thinking about the situation, I came to the conclusion that I would not only take her to her cousin, but plead for Helen to stay in their lands. She would be safe there, and from what my men gathered about his bride, she was forgiving and kind. This gave me the assurance that she would forgive Helen of her trespasses, which were so small in comparison to mine.

I went to bed thinking, hoping Nor would come sooner than later since my heart was already grieving her being gone. Time would only make it worse. Grateful that when morning came, it seemed fate heard my plea.

Chapter 23

HELEN

I couldn't believe my ears. I woke up to Mrs. Lynn talking about how Prince Devron wanted to see me immediately, that his commander just came back with good news.

Only realizing I was now in my bedroom and that Devron must have carried me back when I accidentally fell asleep in his arms. My heart was so full as Mrs. Lynn helped me dress. Things were turning around, and it was all thanks to Devron.

"Oh, deary, must you fidget so. I can barely get these hairs up and out of your face when you're as jumpy as a bean."

"Oh, Mrs. Lynn, I'm so sorry. I'm just so excited to hear the news."

"Ah, that should do it. Now, don't be messing up my work, ya here? Oh, come give me a hug. Good news is always a song to the ears around these parts. Oh, the days when the queen was alive." Then she looked at me with raised eyebrows and a knowing smile on her face. "Maybe they'll be like that once again." I flushed with pleasure at her words.

"I don't....I..." I didn't know what to say, while I knew I cared for Devron, no, I loved him. It was true. My heart yearned to be his and only his. I did not know how it would work, though, but today was not a day to dwell on such thoughts. Devron's commander returned and I anticipated what news he brought.

Mrs. Lynn led me to the Throne room, where I entered seeing the prince talking with the commander and his captain. Devron turned to me as I approached them. Meeting me halfway he wrapped one arm around my waist, securing me to his side, as he led me towards his men.

Nor's eyebrows were raised and a knowing smile was on his face, and I flushed at being caught in the prince's arms. My gaze caught the captains, who had a look of displeasure, making me feel out of place. Turning back to Devron, I noticed he had a scowl of disapproval for his captain, and his grip tightened around my waist. A sense of security came over me at Devron's defense of me. His captain straightened and Nor cleared his throat at the interaction between the captain and his prince. He then proceeded with the news.

"We found them in a far-off village, in the kingdom of Tren. They've been traveling with a caravan for years. It seems they still don't remember where they are from or any family connections."

The commander then looked at me with regret. "I'm sorry, my lady, If I would have known the connection they had to you, I would have thought twice about the memory spell." Then he bowed before me. "Please forgive me."

My heart softened towards this man as he tried to make up for his mistakes. How could I hold a grudge when I alone needed so much redeeming?

"Of course, commander. I'm just so grateful that you have taken the time to find them. Thank you for all that you both have done. I hope to redeem myself, too in this endeavor. Do you think you could take me to them?"

He looked at the prince, who looked at me.

"They might not remember who you are. Are you sure you are okay with this?"

"Yes. I also need to tell Claira. No matter the consequences, she needs to know."

Devron gave me a nod of approval, and the commander turned and waved his hand in a circular motion, opening a portal to an unknown town. Devron grabbed my hand, and we stepped through.

Chapter 24

HELEN

We stepped out of the portal into a large field filled with caravans. Devron moved his hand around my waist, tucking me close to him. His other hand was on the handle of his sword as he scanned the area. It brought back memories of how recently I was with my mother, going through an encampment of vagabonds to meet this man who was supposed to be my doom. Now, here with him, he was the answer to help me redeem myself. Love filled my whole body for him at the growth we had together in such a short time and how things were finally turning around.

"This way, Your Highness, my lady." Nor led us through the wagons. I noticed a couple up ahead, and my heart pounded in my chest as so many emotions swept through me. They were surrounding a small fire. Their clothes and faces dirty from travel. Thin blankets wrapped around their shoulders as they tried to get warm since their lean frames held no ounce of fat.

Tears streamed down my face at what they must have suffered these last few years. I walked up to them, not knowing what to say or do since Nor said they wouldn't likely remember me.

My aunt turned to me and her eyebrows lifted in surprise, then her lips tightened with worry. My uncle wasn't paying attention as he fiddled with a piece of wood and a small knife. I didn't think it was possible for a heart to break so much since there was no recognition in her eyes of who I was.

"Well, hello there, my darling. You seem lost. Is everything okay?" She stood up and waved me over to sit next to her.

Before stepping towards her I looked back to find Devron and Nor off to the side, no doubt giving me space. I turned back to my aunt and nodded that

I was fine. She motioned for me again to sit next to her on the log.

"What's troubling you?" she asked, wrapping an arm around me. It was so like her. She was always kind and caring, just like Claira. I choked on my tears, grief overcoming me.

She leaned forward, catching my eye and she tilted her head to the side. "Hmmm, you remind me of someone?" I did? Was she beginning to recognize me?

"I do?" Hope filled my voice.

"Yes…oh, but it was so long ago." Then she shook her head and blinked a few times, patting my arm.

"What's your name dear?"

"Helen," I softly told her, wondering if my name would jog a memory as to who she was to me.

"What a pretty name…hmmm, It sounds familiar." She paused thinking on this statement, as if the answer was just out of reach, then shaking her head she continued, "Oh, where are my manners! My name is Melinda, and this is my husband John." She said pointing to my uncle who barely looked up to acknowledge me. "But that doesn't matter" She smiled at me. "Now, why is a girl like you crying? You're too pretty, surely, to have time for such tears."

If she only knew.

"It seems I have lost my way, and I was hoping you could help me."

"Lost your way? You poor dear, of course. Now, you tell me all about it, and I'll see how I can help you."

Where could I even start? That my mother wanted to end your lives, but thankfully those two fae over there saved you, but erased your memory, and that is why you are in this predicament. Let us not forget how I treated your daughter these last five years with resentment.

"It's fine. I'm sure I'll find my way." I nodded and then stood up to leave, I could not handle the guilt that was weighing on me being in their presence. It was time to go.

"Hmmm, now I remember…" I quickly looked back at my aunt. "Yes…you remind me of someone I used to know…someone my daughter used to…" Then her eyes went wide as they looked into the distance, shock overcoming her.

"…Claira…" she breathed in recognition.

Then she turned to me and pulled me into a fierce hug. "Oh, Helen! It's you! Oh, my dear girl! My dear, dear girl" she sobbed and turned me to my uncle.

"John, it's Helen. Helen has found us!" The same recognition came into his eyes, and soon we were all embracing as tears freely flowed between us. I didn't think the spell could be broken, but it seemed fate was on our side.

After there were no more tears to cry. I told them how they came to be here and where Claira was now. I was expecting rebuke, but my aunt's sympathy showed again.

"It is not your fault, dear. I'm sorry what your mother put you through…what she put us all through."

I thought I had no more tears to cry, but her compassion towards me proved it otherwise.

I felt someone come up behind me, and I turned to find Devron smiling down at me. I pulled him towards my aunt and uncle.

"This is his royal highness, Prince Devron, and his commander," I pointed to the tall burley fae who stood afar. "They helped me find you."

"Thank you, your highness. It seems Helen must mean a lot to you to go through such trouble."

Devron looked down at me smiling. "Not at all. Her happiness is mine, and I'm so glad she is finally reunited with you." My heart fluttered at his words. Then turning to my aunt and uncle he continued, "you are welcome to come back with me and wait at my keep until I can reach my cousin, who is the fae married to your daughter. We are not on the friendliest of terms, but no doubt his wife's happiness will outweigh any differences we personally have between us."

"I would be my honor, your highness. Thank you so much." My aunt said. They gathered the few things they had and said goodbye to the friends they had traveled with these last few years, each of them rejoicing in their news.

Stepping away from the Caravan and into the forest, Nor opened a portal leading us back to the keep. Once everyone was through, I took a moment to look back at the encampment where we found my aunt and uncle. For the first time in a long time, my heart felt free of guilt, and I knew it was going to be okay.

Chapter 25

HELEN

"Helen! No!" Devron shouted after I stepped out of the portal and into his throne room.

I was yanked by the arms and pulled back against someone's chest. A scream left my lips only to be silenced as a dagger pressed against my throat. Fear was trembling through me. My eyes shifted around the room to see the situation at hand. Devron was kneeling on the floor, his arms held behind his back by fae guards I did not recognize. Furious rage etched onto his face. I noticed an unconscious body lying in front of him and recognized it as his commander. I quickly scanned for my aunt and uncle. They were huddled together in a corner surrounded by more fae guards, all wearing the same symbol I saw so long ago; a snake wrapped around a sword.

"Oh, she is a pretty little thing, isn't she? Human, too." Came the voice of the man who held me captive.

"Let her go, Kadrell! Your fight is with me! Leave her alone!" Devron roared at him.

"No! You forget your place! You are failing in your duties to your king!"

Panic overcame me as I realized it was the King of the Dark Fae that held me captive. All the stories I have heard over the last couple of weeks, made me shiver with fear.

He continued, "Lucky, I had a man who told me all about your pretty little dealings of late."

Then, a figure stepped into the center of the room. Brenon, the captain of Devron's guard, came and squatted next to his former leader.

"You are weak, and not worthy of leadership!" he spat in the prince's face.

"You traitor!" Devron snarled at his captain, his power whipping around him, causing the guards holding him down to falter. "I trusted you!"

Brenon faltered backward at the surge of power coming off the prince.

The dagger pressed deeper into my throat. "Be careful, little brother, her life is in your hands.

Devron breathed in deeply and hung his head in submissiveness, letting his powers die. The captain snarled at the prince and spat at his feet, then made his way over to stand by the king.

"Good, but I won't let you get off that easily. You need a reminder of who you serve." Nodding to one of his men who came forward with a cat-o-nine tails whip in his hands.

No!

The guard was large and chorded with muscle, a monster to serve the prince's unholy punishment. He lifted the whip high, striking with fervent force against his bare flesh. He cried out in agony, and I wished I could break free and save him from this torture. Tears spilled onto my cheeks and after five strikes I could not stand to watch any longer, my heart breaking with each assault. Three more strikes, and I opened my eyes to see Devron on the ground, trying to catch his breath, his face scrunched up in agonizing pain. Then his eyes closed and his body slumped all the way to the ground, not moving anymore. I held my breath, begging him to show life. He could not be gone. Not after everything we have been through. He moved slightly, and relief went through me, then the guard raised the whip again to strike again.

I must do something!

"Please, please stop." I begged. "I'll do anything, please, just stop." Sobs breaking my composure and pressing the dagger deeper.

I saw the king raise his hand to my right and the guard stepped back at his signal to my relief.

The dagger left my throat, and I breathed in deeply. The king whipped me around, grabbing my hands and holding me in place. He was tall and strong, just like Devron, but with long black hair. His armor shined black to match his heart. A snake-shaped crown sat upon his head. The center held a ruby that was placed between the snake's fangs. He was cruel as he was handsome. This man was terror itself, the realization of what I had just bargained for settled in my soul with horror.

"That can be arranged." A wicked gleam in his eyes. "A life for a life, don't you think?"

I looked to the guard who delivered the prince's punishment and realized the fate I just gave myself.

"No, Helen." Came a raspy cry from Devron. I tilted my head and he was trying to sit up, but his body could not hold him after the brutality it just received, and he fell back to the ground. I wanted to run to him and take us far away from here and this nightmare.

The king grabbed my wrist, pulling me back to face him. Another guard came up to hold my other arm in place. To my relief, the whiplash never came, but instead he took the dagger and made a thin, long, cut along my palm. I sucked my breath in through my teeth at the pain, only imagining what Devron must be suffering. The cut ran crimson, and he then grabbed my hand with his own and started to speak the words I now realized were binding me to this evil man. A life for a life.

A blood bond I form

From me to thee

Life force shared

Servitude for eternity

I immediately felt the invisible chains take place on my body that affirmed I was not my own, but his. Forever. He let me go, his hold strong on me, even though he was no longer touching me.

"It is done."

Then he opened a portal, and I stepped through with him to my sorrowful fate. My choices no longer mine, but before the portal closed I had one last look at Devron and our eyes met as he reached out to me, my heart breaking in two. At least he was safe, for now.

Once I stepped all the way through the portal, I was immediately grabbed and thrown into a large iron cell. Reaching out to stop my fall onto the cold stone floor that was covered with rotting hay, only brought me throbbing pain. I gasped as my newly received cut, from the blood bond, hit the cold sharp stones and shot pain all the way up my arm. I cried out and immediately turned to my backside to cradle my hand to my chest.

The bars between us gave me some courage as the king locked my cell.

"He'll come for me! You think you've won. Just wait, Devron will not let you get away with this!" I shouted at him, praying my words were true, that I eventually would be free from this horrible fate.

A vile smirk formed on his lips.

"Oh, I am counting on it." Then he turned and left me alone in the dark. Wondering what I just bargained for.

I grabbed the hem of my dress and tore off a strip of cloth and hissed in pain as I wrapped it around my palm to help stop the bleeding. My eyes finally adjusted to the darkness as a sliver of moonlight came through a small opening at the top of my cell.

I went to a corner, and moved the rotting hay away with my foot and sat down, bringing my knees to my chest, letting the tears flow as I prayed this nightmare would end. Wondering if this was the punishment the fates seemed fit to bestow upon me for the years of my own cruelty.

Chapter 26

DEVRON

I woke up laying on my stomach, searing pain shooting all throughout my back as I groaned in agony. Memories flooded me as I opened my eyes, trying to sit up. I had to save Helen. Who knows what my brother was doing to her, and the longer I stayed in this bed, the longer she was in danger.

"Easy, Your Highness. You are still recovering." Nor told me from the side of my mattress.

"Oh, that cruel, cruel man." Mrs. Lynn cried then sniffed. "How dare he hurt our prince, I tell you. Then take that dear girl away from us. It's cruel and unforgiving."

I tried to get up again, but my strength was gone. Mrs. Lynn placed a cool cloth on my back and gave me a tonic to drink. Once I finished, I handed it back to her and looked towards Nor with determination.

"I must save Helen. She is in danger, and you know it."

"No, you must rest and recover." Nor stated. "Do you think going in there now with your current condition will do either of you any good? You will never make it out alive, and it will all be for not. If you are to save her, you need to make sure you can get both of you out alive."

He was right, as much as I hated it. I was not fit to barge in and take her back from my brother.

"What happened to her aunt and uncle? Are they still alive?"

"Yes, and recovering from the ordeal. I have placed them in capable hands."

Good. With those thoughts, I decided to close my eyes and rest. The sooner I let my body heal, the sooner I would be able to rescue the girl who not only changed my life, but my heart.

TWO WEEKS LATER

"Are you ready?" I asked Nor, as I strapped my dagger and sword over my leather armor. My wounds have finally healed, only thin scars to remind me of the ordeal. Grateful for my healing powers and the many tonics that helped me along the way. If they were deadly strikes, I might not have made it. Fae magic could only go so far.

"Yes, Your Highness." Then he turned to Joel and Marrin, who were coming with us, to review their orders. They were to stay outside the secret passage that led inside the castle walls. As a young boy, I found them as an escape from my father's wrath. Now, they would help me rescue the girl I love. My guards were to make sure our path stayed clear once we found Helen and brought her back through the passage.

We couldn't open a portal directly into the castle, since that privilege was only given to the king, but since I was royalty, it would allow me and my men onto the castle grounds with no disturbance. The only time I have ever been grateful for my lineage was now.

"Let's go," I ordered. We took out our weapons from their sheaths preparing for anything we may encounter. I opened a portal next to the castle's stone wall that was covered in the black of night. We stepped through and quickly made our way to hide behind the large oak tree that sat in front of a slit in the wall. The hidden opening led to the guards armory, next to the dungeons.

Leaving Joel and Marrin at the entrance, Nor and I squeezed through; our large bodies pressed right up against the stone wall. I made it out first and scanned the area. Luckily, no one was in the armory, only weapons that leaned against the wall. I signaled for Nor to follow, letting him know it was clear. Then twisting my magic around my hand, and with one swipe, I shattered each and every one of the weapons within the room, turning them to dust. Not leaving them to be used as an advantage towards our small rescue party.

I saw a torched light down the hall that led to the dungeons and decided to check there first. One of my brother's men was guarding the entrance. I signaled for Nor to stop as I put a cloaking spell on me and snuck up ahead. My dagger made swift work to remove the obstacle, and my hand over his mouth to muffle any sounds that came from him.

Grabbing the torch and key from the guard's belt, I opened the dungeon doors, and we made our way inside the dark and damp prison.

I was careful not to touch the bars since they were made of iron and iron burned fae, but I would gladly rip them apart if it meant freeing her.

I heard a moan to my right and saw a clumped up figure in a corner. I lifted the torch higher to see if it was her.

"Nor! I found her!" He came rushing to my side from searching the other cells and I handed him my torch. Then, grabbing the keys, I anxiously put them in the lock and turned until I heard the click that signified it was now unlocked. Throwing open the door, I rushed to her side. The light from the torches showed her in a state that made me cry out. She was bruised, and her eyes were hollow. I looked down to her hand and horror overcame me as I saw a piece of her dress wrapped around what could only mean one thing. She was blood-bonded to my brother. Anger like never before surged through me. It was probably the only thing keeping her alive, but he would pay and dearly so.

I picked her up in my arms, her head flopping onto my shoulder, and made my way out of the cell, and turned towards the entrance of the dungeon so we could make a quick escape. I would find a way to break the bond no matter what it took. I was stopped short by the man who caused all this, along with the traitor who stood beside him.

"You're so predictable, little brother." He scoffed, pulling out his own sword. "I've had enough of your games. Let's finish this."

I placed Helen down behind me and nodded to Nor. He was right. "Let's finish this." I snarled back.

Chapter 27

DEVRON

Unsheathing my sword again, I wrapped my power around the weapon, the blue wisps lighting up the metal and lightning sparks forming in my other hand. My brother did the same, his black and dark, just like he was. I stepped towards him, my sword raised to strike with precision. A battle cry escaping my lips, signaling his fate.

He stepped forward and blocked my attack, bringing his sword around to strike again. Dancing around each other with skill and power that added to our blows. Strike after strike our fight continued, both determined to be the winner in our fight to the death. Kadrell eventually pulled back and we circled one another, catching our breaths, my eyes never leaving my opponent. I heard a scream and quickly looked to see my former captain with a dagger in his heart, his sword above his head as if ready to strike.

Out of the corner of my eye, I saw my brother lunge toward me, using my distraction as an advantage. It seemed like time stood still as I brought my sword up to meet my enemy's blow, realizing I was too late to block his attack. Nor was suddenly in front of me, blocking the deadly strike. The sword pierced through his armor, straight into his heart.

He fell back into my arms and shock went through my body as I went to my knees, holding the only man who has ever believed in me against my chest. His breath came out ragged as he slowly turned his head to me, "You've always been… worthy… my prince… never forget that." Then his eyes slowly closed as the last breath left his body.

Power like I never felt before surged through and around my body, creating a dome of protection for my love and loyal commander. Bursting forth with unyielding vigor into the dungeon walls. My grief, pain, and anger giving it fuel. It surged up along the walls cracking the stone frame which made up the castle's prison. Pulsing its way towards my brother, who didn't have a chance to flee. I would not allow it. Years of torment and being a pawn to his games have gone on long enough. I would make sure he never hurt anyone I love. Ever. Again.

This ended now.

Giving my dark power one more pulse of energy, my body throbbing with retribution, that carried the final blow towards the man who betrayed me. The walls came plummeting down on them, creating their own graves below the crumbling castle stone.

I breathed out, my head hanging low. It was finished.

Chapter 28

DEVRON

I could hear feet pounding against the stone floor outside the dungeons and prepared myself to face my brother's loyal guards. Joel and Marrin appeared, to my relief at the crumbled entrance. They climbed over the stone, making their way to me, their eyes going wide as they saw their commander next to me. Their heads hung low as they both kneeled beside him and pressed their fist to their hearts in honor of their commander. Then Joel picked him up and with a nod, headed towards the entrance to take him back home. I made my way back to Helen, who was now being watched over by Marrin.

He looked at me with despair in his eyes.

"I don't think she is going to make it." I pushed past him to see her lips blue, and her body was cold. The only sign of life was the small rise of her chest. He was right, she wouldn't make it out of these walls. I felt helpless. I've lost everything, and for what?

"There is one way." He suggested.

No! Not with her. Anything but that. I looked at her again, my brain wracking with anything else but what he was suggesting. Then her head tilted down, as if life itself were leaving her, and I realized I had no other choice. I quickly unwrapped the cloth that covered her hand, grateful I didn't have to make a cut, and grasped her cold, lifeless fingers, saying the words that would bind her to me. Once spoken, I pushed my life force into her, hoping and praying I wasn't too late. After what seemed like an eternity, her lips started to gain color. Then her eyes fluttered open, and she gave me a small smile. I pulled her to my chest and tucked my head into her neck, breathing her in as tears streamed down my face.

In a small, hoarse voice, she whispered, “I knew you would come.”

Chapter 29

HELEN

I looked around and was back in my room at Devron's castle, laying in bed. Surely, it was a dream, but I would hold onto it as long as I could, not wanting to wake up in the dark and damp dungeon. Here, the pain was gone. Here, I felt safe. The door opened and Mrs. Lynn came bustling in and gave me one look, tears coming to her eyes.

"Oh, blessed be the day, you're awake!" Then she hurried out.

"Wait!" I called to her. I didn't want her to leave, Needing the comfort and kindness she always brought with her presence. Deciding to follow her, I pulled back the blanket, noticing my hand was free of the bandage and only a thin scar remained on my palm. I looked at the scar, turning it back and forth only confirmed that my mind took me to a place where I could escape my torture. I still felt a pull for some reason. It wasn't like the chains the king had bestowed upon me when he bound me to him, more of a pull that gently guided me. *Hmmm?* Wondering why the change.

I was thrown from my thoughts when the door suddenly was thrown open, and Devron stepped in, rushing to my side and pulling me in his arms. Oh, if the dream could last forever. He took my face between his hands, and looked into my eyes before bringing his lips to mine in the most tender and loving kiss. I reached around his neck and pulled him closer to deepen the kiss, my hands going in his hair. Tears streamed down my cheeks, it felt so real, wanting it to be with all my heart.

"Don't leave me, please, Devron, please." I begged him, kissing him between each word. "I don't want this to end. I don't want to go back to that cold place. I want to stay here with you."

He pulled me back and looked at me earnestly. "You are safe Helen, no one will ever hurt you again." Then he pulled me back into his arms and rocked me. "You are safe."

"I don't want this dream to end." I told him, knowing I would wake up soon, I pulled him closer, needing him to know how I felt even if the only prince that knew was a figment of my imagination. Regretting I never actually told him in person.

Then pulling back and taking his face in mine, I told him the words etched in my heart.

"I love you, Devron."

His eyes widened and a broad smile formed on his mouth as he brought his forehead down to touch mine, his hands slipped behind my neck into my hair. "I love you too."

My heart burst at his words, and more tears streamed down my face.

"Why are you crying, love?" He asked, wiping my tears with his thumbs.

"I'm just sad that this will end. I don't want it either. I don't want to wake up in that cold dungeon again without you really knowing how I feel."

He looked confused, then gave me a soft smile.

"Helen, this *is* real. Don't you remember me rescuing you?"

I sat there for a while, contemplating his words. Then it was as if my mind opened and my memories returned. This was real. He was before me and I was safe.

He loved me?

He truly loved me?

If my heart burst before, it couldn't contain it now. Then he grabbed my hand where the scar was and his countenance changed. Regret and worry overcame his features, making me worry. Did he not mean what he said? Maybe I was too eager.

"Helen, I hope that you can forgive me for what I am about to tell you. It was the only way to save your life."

He gently ran over the scar on my palm and looked at me, searching my eyes with apprehension. I cupped his cheek with my other hand.

"Whatever it is, it's okay. Thank you for saving me."

He hung his head. "I hope that is still the case." Then he looked me straight in the eye, "I had to blood bond you to me so I could heal you." I pulled my hand back, shocked at his words.

"What?"

"You were dying, and the only way to save you was to bond you with me and give you my own life force." He grabbed my hand back and pleaded with me. "I'm sorry Helen, it was the only way, but it does not change the way I feel about you. You are my everything, and I will find a way to fix this. I promise you." I believed him. I could feel it.

He then told me all that took place during the rescue.

"You're the next in line then?"

"Yes."

My heart sank knowing he would have to pick someone worthy to rule beside him and I knew I was not fit to be queen. Maybe once we returned my aunt and uncle to my cousin, she would have compassion and let me stay with her. My heart broke at the thought of leaving him, but I knew it was the only way.

He paused and I noticed his eyes were red and lips in a straight line.

"Nor…Nor, gave up his life to save us both."

Tears sprang to my eyes, and my heart reached out to him. His pain becoming my own. I didn't know if the bond made it stronger, or if it was because of the love I felt for this man. The whole situation was so twisted and wrong. Why did it have to turn out this way for us, to be reduced to losing everything we loved.

Two nights later, I stood beside Devron as the flames consumed the commander's body. The most honorable way fae could give tribute to those who have passed into the next life. He was stoic as he faced the flames, grasping his hand in mine as if it was the only thing keeping him bound to this mortal world. I squeezed his hand, showing my support. We stayed there until the flames died, but our grief was much alive.

Chapter 30

2 WEEKS LATER

HELEN

They were expecting us, as Devron made a portal just outside the castle to the Kingdom of Llor, just as we agreed for our meeting today. As we stepped through, we were immediately surrounded by guards. The man who married my friend, Lillian, five years ago was the one who greeted us with swords drawn from his men.

"Let them pass Ronin, they bring good news." The Fae King said to his Commander. He raised his hand, and his guards stepped aside. I saw Claira and Lillian and my heart soared at seeing my friend, and hoped that my cousin would forgive me of my trespasses. Devron stepped forward and bowed and I followed with a curtsey.

"Your majesty, cousin, I have come to you in hopes that though we have not always seen eye to eye, that we can soon unite our kingdoms in alliance once more. I offer a recompense for my actions years ago."

The small guard that followed us, stepped aside to reveal my aunt and uncle.

Claira gasped. "Mama? Papa?"

As they ran to each other I couldn't help the tears that flowed down my own cheeks at seeing their joy of being together once more.

"Helen?" I turned and saw Lillian in front of me, her own eyes glistening. She grasped me in an embrace and shock went through me. I thought she would be cold towards me, knowing how I treated my cousin and her friend.

"Oh Helen, me and Claira were so worried about you."

"About me?" I sobbed in unbelief. It seemed that is all I had been doing the last month was cry, but I couldn't help it.

"Yes, you silly girl. His Majesty explained everything in his letter to King Leon, but even before that, we worried so much about you."

They worried about me? After all I did?

"Oh, Helen!" This time it was Claira as she came up and hugged me tight. "I was worried sick about you. Are you okay?"

My ears must be deceiving me. I pulled back and grabbed her hands, choking on my words. I had to do it now before I could no longer speak.

"Claira, I'm…I'm so sorry for how I treated you. You…you wouldn't believe the torment I've been through the last couple months realizing how wrong I was. Would you…could you ever forgive me?"

She grabbed my cheeks as tears streamed down her face. "There is nothing to forgive." Then we hugged. Our little trio was reunited once more.

"Come, let us go inside. There is much to catch up on."

Hours passed as we sat. Claira catching up with her parents and Lillian telling me about her story with Ronin. It was full of laughter, tears, and such happiness that I hadn't felt in such a long time. I didn't want it to end.

After a while her maids came in announcing it was time to get ready for the ball.

"Ball?" I couldn't help the panic that was in my voice as I looked down at my plain attire.

"Oh, yes, we decided at the last minute it would be a wonderful way to celebrate all that has happened," Claira said with a twinkle in her eye.

"But.."I pointed to my dress, showing them I did not have the proper gown for such an event.

"Oh, don't worry, I have just the thing." Lillian beamed.

Chapter 31

DEVRON

"Well cousin, it seems you are smitten with the girl." My cousin smirked from his seat across from me. We just finished up the last details of our alliance in his private sitting room, but my thoughts kept drifting to Helen.

"Hmmm?" I glanced at him as he pulled me out of my thoughts of the dark-haired beauty somewhere in this castle, no doubt enjoying the luxuries this kingdom's wealth provided. I shook my head, wanting to give her that and more. I had so much to do to restore my kingdom and its people. I wanted her beside me in that endeavor, but how could I ask that of her when she could stay and enjoy those things now with her cousin.

"Don't you need a queen now that you are king?" He asked.

My ears perked at his statement as I turned to him. He laughed aloud and I wondered what he thought was so humorous.

"Don't forget, cousin, it was only a few months ago that I was in your same situation."

Yes, and how those few months have changed my own life.

"Yes, but you don't understand." I turned to him, hesitating to tell him about the blood bond I formed with her.

He sat back raising his eyebrows, and put his hand out offering me to continue. Breathing in deeply I told him the story about me and Helen.

After I finished, he didn't say anything for a while. Regretting I even told him, hoping he would not go back on our alliance after finding out what I had done to the girl. No, it was the only way I could save her life, I would do it all again if I had to. Then he looked up at me and said to my relief, "I believe I can help you with your predicament. There are two ways you can break this bond."

"I'm listening."

We were standing in the ballroom an hour later, waiting for the celebration to start. I didn't realize there would be a ball tonight held on behalf of the queen and her family, and their joyous reunion. Luckily, I was the same build as my cousin, who lent me formal attire for the occasion. My heart was filled with joy and hope as Leon relayed to me earlier on how his father broke the blood bond with his servants. I could not wait to tell Helen.

Standing beside my cousin as he introduced me to many Lords and nobility of his Kingdom, I received many different greetings. Some were suspicious, while others were curious of how the

Dark Fae King came to be here tonight. The ladies still had not arrived yet and I was burning with anticipation, trying not to let it show and be attentive to my cousin's guest before me. I had to start now in showing those that surrounded me that the dark fae have changed. That its current ruler was different from the tyrant my brother was.

A nudge in my side made me glance at Leon who smiled at me and then nodded towards the doors that led into the ballroom across from where we stood. My breath stilled as I looked at the beauty before me, dressed in the colors of my Kingdom. Not even noticing her cousin and friend, who were by her side. Her black dress glistened with rubies as the material shimmered under the light, showing off her figure with grace as it flared out at her knees. I could not take my eyes off of her.

Right then the music started and I was determined to take her in my arms and not let her go the rest of the night. Right as I was about to step down from the platform, my cousin's commander stepped in front of Helen and asked her to dance. Jealousy coursed through me at the impertinence of the man, as he looked back at me with a smug look on his face as he pulled her into his arms and started twirling her around the floor.

"Easy cousin." Leon laughed out loud and slapped me on the back. "He's just trying to rile you up. There will be plenty of dances to hold her in your arms later."

I looked at him and raised an eyebrow, a smirk forming on my face. Two could play this game. "No one said I couldn't do it now." Then I made my way towards the commander. Determined to take back what was mine.

Chapter 32

HELEN

"How are you enjoying yourself, my lady?" Lillian's husband asked me as he twirled me around on the dance floor.

"Wonderful commander, I'm so glad to hear my friend is taken care of and that she has found you. We have worried about her so much, ever since that day five years ago."

"She talked about you often and I know how much you mean to her. Do you plan on staying? Surely, you won't go back with the Dark Fae King?" He said with mischief in his eyes.

I hesitated. It's what I wanted but I didn't know my place just yet within this fae world or what place I held in Devron's life. I knew he loved me but could it ever go beyond that?

"Surely commander, you have better things to do than taunt the lady, such as practice your dancing skills, they seem to be lacking. Do not fret though, they say one dances only as well as they spar."

The commander turned and to my grateful heart, laughed at Devron's taunting. Gently tugging me towards the dark fae king and handing me off to his outstretched hand. I placed my hand in his, his eyes burning as they gazed into mine, my hand tingling where he gently pulled me to him. The commander bowed and gracefully let Devron cut into our dance as he made his way over to his wife.

Suddenly, I became aware that it was just me and him, and my skin flushed with heat. I tipped my head down to break the eye contact, he looked striking in his formal attire. He placed a finger under my chin and gently tilted my face back up to his.

"You look beautiful, Helen." His eyes burning with desire.

"Thank you." I softly replied, my heart pounding out of my chest at his intense gaze. Then he pulled me so close to him, there was no space between us as he led me into the waltz around the room. As he twirled me around, I felt so free. Freer than I have felt in a long time.

"I have found a way to set you free from our bond." My heart sank at his words, while I understood the bond was one of servitude, he did not treat me as such, and it was the last connection that I had to this man.

"I understand." Knowing this could never last forever, he needed someone who could rule by his side forever. I was just a mere human girl, whose life was short compared to his immortal existence.

He stopped our dancing and pulled me behind him, making our way through the guests, leading me out onto the balcony and down the stairs to sit on a stone bench in the garden. No one was here as far as I could tell. He didn't say anything at first so I looked around at the magnificent gardens before me. They were unlike anything I have ever seen before. Magical was the only word to describe it. Lanterns had flowers wrapped around its poles and bulbs floating in the air. Light sparkled like stars, giving an enchanting look to enhance the splendor before us.

"It's beautiful," I whispered.

"Yes, it is." I turned to see him staring at me, and I flushed at his meaning.

Then he looked around the gardens with scrutiny.

"I would understand if you wanted to stay here." He sounded sad, so I turned to him.

"What do you mean?" I said, grabbing his hand to confront him.

"Over a thousand years ago my uncle found a way to break the blood bond. Leon told me."

Then he turned to me with all seriousness. "You could stay here and be free. You could live a life of luxury with your cousin and dearest friend. You don't want me, Helen. My kingdom is broken. I can't offer you all that Llor can."

I wish he would stop. He was all I wanted, I didn't care about his lands or wealth, but the man who truly loved me, or I thought he did, but I was speechless as he continued, my heart breaking with every word. Reality sunk in that maybe he didn't want me since he was offering me a way out.

"You would never want for anything. You could traverse these beautiful gardens every night and have many lords and noblemen..."He paused as he struggled to get the next words out. "Who would ask for your hand."

I didn't want any of them. Did he not know he was the only one who I wanted in my life?

"What are you saying, Devron?" I tried to ask calmly but the tremble in my voice deceived me.

"That you could stay here if you wanted…without me… if that is what you wish."

I didn't know how to respond and tears betrayed me as they slipped down my cheeks so I asked him a question instead.

"And what is it *you* want?"

Then he pulled me to him and caressed my cheeks, wiping the tears away.

"Helen, all I want is you." Then he tenderly kissed me on the lips, but I was so confused.

"But you said…"

"There is another way if you will have me, Helen. The Sacred Bonding Ritual among the fae, that will unite us as husband…" His eyes burned into my soul with longing, "and wife."

My breath caught in my throat. Was he?

"You wish to…to marry me?"

"If you'll have me."

I flung my arms around his neck and kissed him passionately, which he returned eagerly. My hands reached up to his hair, as his arms wrapped around my waist, pulling me closer. We came up for a breath, my heart soaring. I looked deep into his eyes and answered, "It is the only way I would ever be bound to a dark fae prince."

Then I kissed him again, knowing I would be his forever.

Thank you to my readers! I hope you enjoyed the ending to Helen and Devron's story!

It doesn't end there though!

A prequel

A Wager for a Bride (A prequel) is the love story of Ronin and Lillian.

Amy Horikami
A Wager
For a
Bride

Made in the USA
Columbia, SC
06 July 2025

60383294R00143